BRIDGE TO BURN

A DETECTIVE KAY HUNTER MYSTERY

RACHEL AMPHLETT

SAXON
PUBLISHING

For Doreen,
who shared my love of reading

ONE

Spencer White took a final drag on the cigarette, dropped the butt to the gutter and slammed the back door of his panel van.

A muscle spasm clutched at the base of his spine as he bent over to pick up his toolbox. He hissed through his teeth, expelling the last of the nicotine-heavy smoke.

Late frost sparkled on the pavement where the sun's weak rays failed to reach into the shadows, and a biting wind tugged at the collar of his waterproof coat. Rainclouds threatened on the horizon, and he shivered.

Shouldering the weight of an aluminium ladder over one arm, the toolbox clutched in his other hand, he waited until a single decker bus shot past him on the busy Maidstone street and then hurried across the road to the newly refurbished office block.

He had been pleased with the call-out. The redevelopment works in the town centre had drawn to their natural completion, and the amount of work he was doing on a weekly basis started to return to its previous levels once the winter months had set in and the hot summer months faded from the memories of the local populace.

He peered up at the façade of the building, squinting against the low morning sunlight.

Once an old bank, the ragstone brickwork now housed a software company. He recalled the number of hours he had spent working late over the summer, as the construction manager for the redevelopment had juggled the completion of the ducted air-conditioning alongside the critical electrical wiring and cabling that was the hub of the business.

It wasn't often that he was asked to return once practical completion had been reached. Most of his income was generated through day-to-day servicing of existing systems. Spencer prided himself on the quality of his work and that of his employees, but accepted that now and again an anomaly could arise and he would do all he could to ensure the problem was fixed as soon as possible.

He propped the ladder against the stone door frame and pressed the button on the security panel to his right. Through the glass, a head bobbed up from behind the reception desk and a buzzing noise reached his ears. The receptionist pushed back her chair and wandered over to the double doors, smiling as she opened one side.

'Thanks,' said Spencer.

'No problem. I'm just glad you could get here so quickly.' She wrinkled her nose, highlighting her freckles. 'It's all very well working in a posh place like this, but not when it's stuffy. It's not like we can open the window or anything.'

Spencer smiled as he picked up the ladder and waited while she let the door swing shut.

He'd been surprised when he'd seen the architect's drawings for the redevelopment of the bank – rather than introduce windows that could be opened now that the building's old use was no more, reverse cycle air-conditioning had been installed instead and the windows resealed to avoid potential burglaries.

He realised it was the lifeblood of his business, but knew he wouldn't be able to face working in such a stuffy environment.

It seemed the software company's employees

were discovering the same for themselves.

'Am I right in thinking the main conduit for the wiring is in the downstairs eating area?' he said.

'That's what Marcus, our operations manager, told me. I'm Gemma, by the way. I'd imagine this place looks a lot different from when you last saw it.'

He glanced around at the brightly painted walls and the modernist artwork that depicted shapes and colours but no real form. 'Just a bit.'

'Give me two seconds. I need to get someone to answer the phones for me, and then I'll show you through. Sign in and help yourself to one of those visitors passes.'

Spencer leaned the ladder against the reception desk and placed the toolbox at his feet, then reached out for the guestbook and scrawled his name in the space provided while Gemma picked up the phone and spoke to a colleague in a low tone.

She replaced the receiver with a smile on her face. 'Okay, all sorted. The phones are diverted so I don't need to worry about those. Come on – hopefully you can sort this quickly. I don't think I can cope with one more phone call from the top floor moaning about it.'

Her heels clacked across the high sheen of the tiled floor before she held open a solid wooden door and stood to one side to let him through.

As Spencer's eyes adjusted from the brightness of the reception area to the subdued hues of the software company's working environment, he couldn't help but feel that the large room now seemed cluttered – there were so many groups of desks and chairs, it was hard to recall the enormous space that he had worked in over the summer.

Even the high ceilings had been lowered and disguised by acoustic tiles that masked the maze of wiring that he himself had been partly responsible for.

He heard a gentle *swish* as the door closed behind him, and then Gemma gestured across the room to an open area beyond.

A waft of roasting coffee beans teased his senses as they made their way around the perimeter before advancing on a space in the middle that included a small kitchenette and a seating area where employees could take a break. Spencer tried to ignore the sweet aroma of fresh doughnuts in case his stomach roared in protest, and bit back a smile at the sight of the state-of-the-art coffee machine. His wife had been nagging him for one like it but he couldn't see the sense in spending that sort of money when it only cost a couple of quid for a jar of the stuff from the supermarket.

Eight men and women milled about, chatting

between themselves in low voices as they opened refrigerator doors, fetched milk cartons and handed out china plates and mugs.

'Bad timing, I'm afraid,' said Gemma. 'Those who come in early usually take a coffee break and grab a bite to eat about now.'

'That's okay,' said Spencer. 'I'll only need to open one of the ceiling panels to start off with. I'll put a couple of chairs out to block off access. No sense in disturbing everyone until I find out what the problem is.'

He noticed her shoulders relax a moment before she let out a breath he didn't realise she had been holding.

'Oh, that's great. Thank you – I was expecting some grief from this lot if I had to tell them to move out of the way. Do you want a coffee or anything while you're working?'

'I'd love a coffee, thanks. Milk, two sugars.'

Spencer set the ladder against one of the Formica tables that were spread about the area then spun three of the chairs around. He opened his toolbox and pulled out the drawings for the air-conditioning wiring that his wife had printed off for him that morning, before glancing at the ceiling as he got his bearings.

'Here you go.'

He swung round at Gemma's voice, then reached out for the steaming mug of coffee she passed to him. 'Thanks. Back behind the chairs now.'

He winked and waited until she'd joined her colleagues at a table two sets away, then turned his attention to the drawings as he took a sip of his drink.

Satisfied he had the right panel, he placed the coffee mug on the table and then bent down to his toolbox, focused on the task at hand.

He whistled under his breath as he worked; a tune that had been playing on the radio that morning when the kids were getting ready for school, his younger daughter annoying her sister by dancing around singing the current hit single at the top of her voice, and now it was stuck in his head.

Spencer straightened and ignored the curious glances from the breakfasting staff. He needed to concentrate; to find the fault, fix it with as little fuss as possible, and try to ensure that whatever was wrong didn't impact his profit on the original job.

He pulled the ladder closer, placed the tools on the table, and then climbed up the first four rungs and pressed his palms against the acoustic tile.

It held fast, refusing to leave the thin strip of aluminium housing that it sat against.

Spencer grimaced, repositioned his hands, and pushed again.

The ladder wobbled under his weight, sending his heart hammering before he glanced down.

'Hang on, I'll hold it for you.'

One of the men shoved his chair away from the far table and hurried over, placing his foot on the base.

'Thanks.'

'No problem. They're nuts about health and safety here, so it wouldn't do us any good if we sat and watched you fall.'

He gave a cheeky smile, and Spencer rolled his eyes.

'You'd think with all the money they spent on this place, they'd have made sure the floor was level down here,' he said.

The man laughed, then placed a hand on the side of the ladder as Spencer turned his attention back to the ceiling.

He frowned, casting his gaze across the panels to the left and right of the one he needed to access, then braced himself and shoved hard.

He caught a smell emanating from the crack that appeared; a reminder of a dead rat that had got locked in a garden shed when he was a kid –

and then the acoustic tile snapped back into place.

He swore, and the man below him chuckled.

Spencer said nothing, and instead placed his right foot on the next rung, repositioned himself and tried again.

His left fist disappeared through the ceiling a split second before a roar enveloped him as the tile disintegrated, destroying the two each side of it.

He fell from the ladder, a cry of alarm escaping from his lips as he tumbled backwards onto the man below in a shower of dust and broken tiles.

Spencer grunted as the wind was knocked from his lungs the moment his shoulders hit the linoleum floor, and then a heavy weight bounced across his legs before falling away.

He lay for a moment, flexing his fingers and toes, making sure he hadn't done serious damage to himself and then coughed to clear the white cloying dust from his mouth and lungs. He blinked, wiping at his eyes with the back of his hand and wondered why his ears were ringing.

As he sat upright, he swallowed.

His hearing was fine, but two of the women who had been in the kitchen when he arrived were on their feet, their food and drinks forgotten.

One held on to Gemma, whose mascara had blotted leaving streaks over her cheeks.

They were all screaming.

Spencer twisted around, thinking that his unofficial assistant had been injured, but when he turned the man was already on his feet, his eyes wide and his face paling to a sickly grey.

'You okay?' said Spencer.

'I think I'm going to be sick,' came the response. He pointed behind Spencer.

Spencer glanced over his shoulder, and then shuffled away as fast as his hands and feet could move, trying to put as much distance as possible between him and the thing that lay slumped beside his ladder.

As his brain began to digest what it was seeing and he fought to keep bile from escaping his lips, all he could recall was that it shouldn't be here, shouldn't be lying on the floor like that, and he needed to get away from it.

The women's screams had subsided to hysterical sobbing as more and more of the staff hurried over from their desks to find out what was going on.

Gemma's voice reached Spencer as he grabbed hold of the back of a chair and hauled himself unsteadily to his feet.

'Why was there a dead man in the ceiling?'

TWO

'Lucky charm,' said Gavin Piper, and led the way along the pavement and towards Gabriel's Hill.

'What?' Detective Inspector Kay Hunter zipped her fleece before hurrying to catch up with the detective constable who kept a rapid pace over the uneven surface. 'And slow down, will you? I know these cobblestones have been replaced, but it's still bloody slippery.'

Gavin paused to let a group of teenagers pass, and then continued. 'Lucky charm. A few hundred years ago, they used to shove a cat into the wall of a building before sealing it as a way to scare off evil spirits. It's like that, isn't it? Mummified.'

'I don't think our victim was put there for luck, Piper.' Kay suppressed a shiver as they reached the crest of the hill. 'No guessing which building is our crime scene.'

Diagonally across from where they stood, two patrol cars and an ambulance hugged the kerb while a silver four-door car had been parked haphazardly, covering half the pavement. A uniformed officer by the name of PC Toby Edwards directed an elderly couple away from the blue and white crime scene tape that fluttered in a cold breeze as Kay and Gavin approached.

'Lucas got here fast,' she said, eyeing the silver car.

'Apparently he was already in town. Conference at the Marriott or something.'

The Home Office pathologist would have been summoned by the first responders, and Kay was glad to have him on site to hear his initial thoughts on the unusual find.

A grey panel van slid to the kerb behind the silver car, and four figures emerged before donning protective outerwear and collecting a range of coloured boxes from the van.

Kay nodded in greeting to the shortest of the four figures and followed Gavin over to where Harriet Baker divided up her small team and sent them towards the building.

'Morning, Kay.' The crime scene investigator shook hands with both of them and lowered her voice. 'I hear we've got a strange one this morning.'

'Apparently so. Gavin and I were on our way in.' Kay shrugged. 'I was at headquarters when the call came through, so I probably know as much as you at the moment.'

'Mummified, I heard?'

'Yes. Lucas is here.'

'Ah, good. Always useful when a pathologist can see a body in situ.' Harriet turned and picked up a box of equipment from the foot-well of the passenger seat of the van. She locked the vehicle and then pulled out a pair of protective gloves, tugging them over her fingers. 'I'd best get on.'

'We'll see you in there.'

Kay stood aside as Harriet swept past and then narrowed her eyes as a familiar figure hurried towards the tape, his focus on the open satchel slung over one shoulder. She called over to the police constable. 'Edwards – make sure Jonathan Aspley doesn't speak to any of the witnesses, would you?'

'Will do, guv.'

The reporter from the *Kentish Times* pulled a phone from his pocket, his gaze locking with Kay's as he neared, then his shoulders slumped as he caught sight of Edwards approaching.

'Oh, come on, Hunter!'

She held up a hand. 'No, Jonathan. Later. Be at headquarters at five o'clock this afternoon. DCI Sharp is organising a press conference. You should get an email within the hour. In the meantime, let my team do their work.'

She turned her back to him before he could protest further. 'Have the paramedics finished?'

'Still with one of the employees,' said Edwards. 'She's asthmatic, and they were concerned about the effect of the shock on her.'

'All right. Extend the cordon a car length beyond the ambulance and get some barriers across the pavement to give us some privacy.' She glanced up at the building opposite, her top lip curling at the sight of a number of inquisitive office workers at windows, smartphones in hand. 'And for goodness sakes get a couple of officers over there to tell that lot to mind their own business.'

'Guv.'

Edwards hurried away, barking orders to his colleagues and relaying Kay's instructions.

Kay moved so she could see past Gavin and down the High Street towards the old Town Hall. Along the length of pavement on each side of Market Square, people stopped and stared. A mixture of curious glances and openly eager faces greeted her, and she knew from experience that it would only be a matter of time before a crowd began to gather, especially if the office workers opposite had already managed to film anything of interest and upload it to social media.

If they didn't manage the situation properly, the town centre would soon be reduced to gridlock.

Running feet drew her attention back to the taped-off perimeter in time to see four uniformed officers hurry across the street and into the building.

'At least they haven't got the body on camera,' Gavin muttered.

'Thank goodness. Who's got the clipboard, Debbie?' said Kay, calling out to a female officer who hovered at the doorway to the software company's premises, several metres away from where they stood.

'Aaron, guv,' said Debbie. 'He's had to give Sergeant Hughes a hand with the barrier. Won't be a minute.'

Despite her impatience at wanting to enter the crime scene, even Kay's rank wouldn't stand her in good stead if she broke with protocol and lifted the tape that stretched between a lamp-post and a gutter bolted to the ragstone brickwork.

'What else do we know about this morning's events?' she said to Gavin, lowering her chin until she sensed the soft fabric of her jacket, then exhaling to create a warm cocoon of air to offset the morning chill.

'No-one knew the body was there until it fell through the ceiling, guv. Apparently, a fault in the ducted air conditioning was reported last week and the bloke who installed it – Spencer White – couldn't get here until today.'

'What sort of fault?' said Kay.

'The system packed up. No air going through the building at all. Being an old bank, and given the amount of traffic that goes by here every day, the windows can't be opened – they're double glazed and sealed. Someone decided to turn up the temperature last week after we had that cold snap, and everything ground to a halt.'

'Bloody hell. So does anyone know how long it was up there?'

Gavin shook his head. 'No, but the acoustic tiles were installed towards the end of the redevelopment works to the building so he wasn't up there before that—'

He broke off and jerked his chin over Kay's shoulder.

Turning, she saw Aaron Baxter approaching, a clipboard in his hand.

'Sorry, guv. Bedlam at the moment.'

'No problem,' said Kay. 'The main thing is, you're maintaining a good crime scene so don't worry about us having to wait.'

The police constable managed a smile as he took back the signed paperwork from Gavin. 'Thanks, guv.'

Kay ducked under the tape Aaron held aloft, waited for Gavin to join her and then took a set of protective coveralls from Patrick, one of Harriet's assistants, and donned the bootees and gloves he held out.

Once suitably attired, she followed Gavin to the front door of the building, noting with relief that the barriers had been erected and the bystanders now moved away from the opposite office block.

The double doors to the old bank had been propped open and as Kay entered, a faint sound of weeping reached her ears.

A young woman, no more than twenty, sat in one of the leather seats in the reception area, a paper tissue clutched in her fist while a colleague tried to placate her.

Debbie moved to Kay and Gavin's side. 'Gemma

Tyson,' she said in a low voice. 'Receptionist. She was present when the victim was discovered.'

Kay nodded her thanks, then moved towards the doors that she reasoned led into the bowels of the building. 'We'll have a quick word with her on the way out.'

Gavin nodded in understanding, then paused as they entered the open plan office. 'Bloody hell.'

The central space that served as the working hub of the software business teemed with people.

A group of a dozen uniformed officers milled about the room. They had divided the employees into small groups in order to seek witness statements from them and ensure mobile phones were confiscated until any photographs were removed and ground rules regarding social media had been communicated.

An air of shock permeated the air, tinged with a dark undertone of disbelief at the sudden entrance of the mummified body.

As they made their way towards the kitchen area and Harriet's team of crime scene investigators who were beginning to process the evidence, Kay fought down the urge to panic at the sheer number of people that were present.

As crime scenes went, it was going to be one of

the hardest to manage and would test her team's skills to the limit.

'What made them suspect foul play?' she said.

'Bloody great dent in the side of his skull,' said Gavin. 'You could say it's a no-brainer, guv.'

Kay groaned, and brushed past one of Harriet's assistants. 'You've got to stop hanging around with Barnes, Piper. He's a bad influence.'

THREE

Kay's newly-appointed detective sergeant had a reputation for his sense of humour but Ian Barnes was an integral part of her team and despite her words, she knew he could show brevity and professionalism when required.

Right now, he was wearing a set of coveralls and was surrounded by people in varying states of preparedness.

Crime scene investigators milled around where the mummified corpse had dropped through the ceiling, while a third police cordon was being established closer to the body.

Barnes glanced up from his notes, acknowledged Kay and Gavin with a nod, then turned his attention to a young uniformed constable and her colleague before pointing towards the far end of the room.

The two officers sprung to action, leaving Barnes to speak with a tall man in a suit who ran his hand through his hair repeatedly as he listened.

'Who's he?' said Kay.

'Managing director, guv,' said Debbie. 'Works on the floor above. In the room above, to be more precise.'

'Has that been taped off as well?'

'Yes. Two of Harriet's team went up there when they arrived, and we've got people speaking to the employees on that floor as well. Thought we'd do it there to keep them away from all this.'

Plastic chairs lay strewn over the linoleum tiles from where they had been shoved backwards by the staff members trying to leave the area in a hurry, and Kay ran a practised eye across the assembled throng that mingled next to a water dispenser over by the far wall.

'Anyone leave?' she said.

'No. All present and accounted for,' said Debbie. 'We won't release anyone from the scene until you say so.'

'Good, thanks. How are you doing, Ian?' said Kay as she drew nearer.

'Good, guv. Hang on.'

He turned and spoke to a uniformed sergeant, and then moved across to where Kay and Gavin stood at the boundary between the office space and the break area, an expression of disgust clouding his features once he was close.

'Never had one like this before,' he said with a shudder. 'First time for everything, I suppose.'

'Looks like you've got it all under control.'

A sense of pride filled Kay as she spoke.

Barnes's decision to apply for the role of detective sergeant had been a surprise to her and others. He had spent the summer shying away from the opportunity only to change his mind at the last minute rather than have a complete stranger join the team.

Kay had been relieved; she enjoyed working with the older detective who had become a good friend as well as a colleague, and someone she could rely upon without having to ask.

He seemed to be thriving on the challenges his role brought, especially now.

Kay craned her neck, but couldn't see past the crime scene investigators who were now crouched on the floor amongst the tables. 'Where's Lucas?'

'Here.'

She spun around at the voice, and came face to

face with the pathologist, his expression weary as he dried his hands on a crunched up sheet of paper towel before placing it in a bag and handing it to a passing CSI team member.

They shook hands, and then she gestured to the area below the gaping hole in the ceiling.

'Can you tell me anything new?'

'That heatwave we had in the summer preserved the body,' said Lucas, keeping his voice low in order to avoid being overheard by the office staff that were being corralled from the water dispenser towards a group of desks. 'I understand these acoustic tiles were installed in late June so whoever hid the body managed it between then and when the building was leased in early October.'

Gavin looked up at the gaping hole leading to the ceiling cavity. 'How on earth do you get a body up there? It'd take more than one person, wouldn't it?'

'Some of Harriet's team are upstairs. They've started pulling apart the office above this,' said Lucas. He beckoned to Harriet. 'Got a second?'

'If you're quick,' said the CSI lead.

'I was going to update Kay with what you're up to, but figured it'd make sense for her to hear it from you in case you already had more information,' said Lucas.

'Okay, yes. We're working on two theories based on what we've managed to ascertain upon arrival. One, the body was raised up into the ceiling from here, or two – whoever did this put the body in the floor of the office upstairs,' said Harriet. 'It wouldn't have been easy pushing our victim up through the ceiling – too heavy for a start, and no way of securing it there until the acoustic tiles had been replaced. Obviously, we'll be able to tell you more as we go but I'm inclined to think it was lowered into the floor above. As the body dried out it shifted through the floor until it was resting on the acoustic tiles and compressed the supply from the air conditioning pipework.'

'Thanks.' Kay turned back to Lucas. 'Do we know if it's male or female?'

'Male, definitely. Do you want to take a look before we move him?'

'I'd better.'

If she were honest, Kay would rather not inspect the mummified body but she knew from experience that if a chance occurred to see a body where it had been discovered, it would often give her more information than she'd glean from reading the stark text of a report, and in her new role as detective inspector she was determined to lead her team by example.

If any of them saw her cutting corners in an investigation, she'd never forgive herself.

'Pop your mask on,' said Lucas. 'We don't know what spores it might be giving off.'

Kay did as she was told. Once she had ensured Gavin donned his mask as well, she followed Lucas and Harriet under the secondary cordon and across the linoleum floor to where the CSIs worked.

At first, the curled-up form on the ground resembled a bundle of rags that that been dropped in a heap but as she drew closer, Kay could make out a clenched hand poking out from a blue shirt sleeve.

Lucas led her around the victim's body, his movements respectful as he dropped to a crouch and gestured to the man's face.

Kay swallowed, then joined the pathologist.

She ran her gaze over the puckered skin of the victim's face.

His eyelids were missing, exposing empty sockets, and his lips were pulled back in an agonised grimace.

'I'm afraid rodents got to his eyes and lips,' said Lucas. 'They don't take long to find a way into a place if they can smell a body, even somewhere like this that's relatively new.'

'Gavin mentioned there's a blunt trauma wound to the head.'

'Yes, here.' Lucas used his little finger to indicate a dent in the victim's skull, behind the left ear. 'I can't say for certain if that's the cause of death until I've had a chance to examine him properly, though.'

'Any identification? Wallet?'

'No, nothing in his pockets.'

'How on earth will you identify him?' said Gavin, his face gradually returning to its normal colour. 'I mean, his face is beyond recognition, and his skin's all wrinkled.'

'We'll get him back to the morgue and try some glycerine on the fingertips to start with,' said Lucas. He cast a sorrowful gaze at the crumpled body. 'That might soften the skin enough to obtain fingerprints to send through to you so you can try to identify him. I can't promise anything for a few days though.'

Kent's post mortems, if not conducted at a hospital where a patient died, were carried out at Derwent Valley hospital by Lucas and a team of morticians who worked in cramped laboratories and were under constant pressure. Added to their workload were the effects of the colder months, with poor weather conditions and fatal cases of pneumonia amongst the older population, so that a post mortem report for a criminal case could take several days at best – sometimes weeks.

'No staining to the ceiling tiles?' said Kay.

'Dehydration would have occurred prior to putrefaction,' said Lucas. 'There must have been enough air flow in the cavity to speed up the process.'

'And no-one would've picked up on any residual smell because the place was empty for two months after the renovations were complete,' said Barnes. 'We've got a copy of the lease agreement, and this lot didn't move in until October.'

'Do we know who the carpet fitters were?'

Barnes jerked a gloved thumb over his shoulder. 'The managing director phoned his operations manager – he's on annual leave at the moment but he's going to go through his files online and email us the details. Local company by the sounds of it.'

'Okay, good.' Kay rose to her feet and cast her gaze around the crime scene. 'All right, Ian. You've got everything under control here. We'll head back to the station and make sure the incident room is ready.'

FOUR

'Hell of a way to start a Monday, guv.'

Detective Sergeant Carys Miles handed Kay a manila folder as she walked into the incident room and headed towards her desk.

'Tell me about it.' Kay shrugged off her fleece and threw it over the back of her chair before flipping open the file. 'What have you managed to find?'

Carys leaned against the desk opposite and hitched a lock of black hair behind her ear as Kay sat. 'The building was owned by one of the big high street banks until the recession a few years ago. It's been leased on a short-term in the years since, but when the last tenant moved out, the owners decided to take advantage of the redevelopment works going on around here and sold the property.'

'They must've made a pretty penny.'

'You're not wrong. The estimated figures are on page four. The new owner – a property development company based in Rochester – contracted out the work. We've collated a list of business names relating to the building from the internet and I'll get some help working through those to find out how they're linked. Some are sole traders, others are limited companies.'

'Barnes is waiting to hear from the current tenant's operations manager,' said Gavin. 'Hopefully he's got a note of the carpet fitters to save you trying to locate them.'

'That'd be good,' said Carys. 'I'm hoping everything's been done by the book and we don't have to worry about cash-in-hand jobs.'

Kay ran her eyes over the text as she flipped through the thin file, then handed it back to Carys.

'This is a good start, thanks.' She checked her watch. 'Who's managing the HOLMES database?'

'Phillip Parker,' said Carys. 'Debbie was rostered out with uniform over the weekend and won't be free until Thursday to join us.'

'Yes, we saw her at the scene. That's okay – Phillip's more than capable of managing it in the meantime. Who else have we got?'

Kay listened and let her gaze wander across the incident room as Carys ran through the names of uniformed officers who had been drafted in to assist her small team of detectives, her heart rate beginning to steady after the adrenalin spike of attending the crime scene.

Her eyes fell upon PC Derek Norris balancing on a chair as he pulled down pale blue paper streamers from the ceiling, and her heart ached.

The previous Friday, one of the administrative staff had brought in her weeks-old baby boy to introduce him to her colleagues and the room had been used as a temporary space to hold a small party for her. Kay had attended, but had drawn worried glances from her fellow detectives. She still felt the pain of loss from her miscarriage some years before, and had found it difficult when the baby had been thrust into her arms and the infant's vivid blue eyes had gazed up at her.

She battened down the memory as Norris climbed from the chair and threw the last of the streamers into the wastepaper basket under the desk, restoring the incident room to its normal practical setting.

Her frozen fingertips began to thaw in the warmth from the central heating that, this winter at least, was working and she reached out gratefully for the mug of tea that Sergeant Harry Davis thrust at her before he headed off towards a desk near the window. She smiled; the older uniformed officer had become quite a father figure to a number of the staff over the years and she always enjoyed his company, even when she was at the beginning of an investigation that would certainly test all her skills as a detective and manager. At least Harry could be relied upon to corral the younger team members when needed.

An air of efficiency filled the room as personnel settled at temporary desks, answered phones and called across to each other – a focus that wouldn't be broken until their victim had been identified and the circumstances of his death resolved.

Carys broke off as the door swung open and Barnes strode towards them, loosening his tie.

'Right, Tutankhamun's off to the morgue and there's a uniform patrol staying at the premises until Harriet's team release the crime scene,' he said. 'What have I missed?'

Kay handed Carys's notes to him, then turned to Gavin. 'Can you get onto the council and find out if there were any issues during the renovation works? Complaints, problems with permits, anything like that.'

'Will do, guv.' He held up his mobile. 'I'll

download the photos I took of our victim and the crime scene too, and get those in the system. Do you want a couple of printouts for the board?'

'Please. Might as well show everyone here what we're up against when it comes to identifying this one. I can't imagine we'll get anything through from Harriet's team until some time tomorrow, not if they're still there.'

Gavin shot off towards his desk and Barnes handed the folder to Carys.

'What are your initial thoughts?' said Kay.

'Well, he obviously pissed off someone,' said Barnes. 'Given the way his skull was broken.'

Carys frowned. 'We haven't had any reports of trouble during the redevelopment works around here. I presume there's no way he could've tripped and fallen into the cavity by accident and banged his head, then?'

'No – we took a look upstairs before we left, and he was definitely hidden on purpose,' said Kay. 'There are all sorts of joists and wiring underneath the mezzanine level. All that would've had to have been moved to one side for him to fit.'

She pushed herself out of her chair. 'Come on – round up everyone and let's have a quick run through what we need to do before the end of today. I need to brief Sharp before he leaves for the press conference in an hour.'

Her stomach rumbled as she reached across for her mobile phone, and Carys rolled her eyes.

'Not a word. I'll eat later,' said Kay.

She moved to the front of the room and waited while her colleagues wheeled chairs across to where she stood next to a whiteboard while Gavin hurried over from the printer.

'Got the photos,' he said, and began to pin up two he'd chosen from those he'd taken.

Kay cleared her throat. 'Settle down, everyone. Let's get on with it.'

A few stragglers hurried to lean against desks or perched on the windowsills, and then she began.

'For those of you who have joined us for the first time today, you'll find we're a close-knit team who like to get things done. Having said that, none of us bites so don't be afraid to ask a question. You might be the one who sets us off in the right direction to get a result, all right?' She smiled as a couple of young constables visibly relaxed and others gave Barnes and the other detectives a knowing nod, before she turned and rapped her knuckles on the first photograph. 'We have a mummified body that was discovered when it fell through a ceiling in the old bank up on the High

Street earlier this morning. No-one was injured, but as you can imagine it was a shock to everyone present.'

A murmur filled the room as the investigative team leaned as one towards the photographs with their notebooks out and pens poised.

'No-one knows who he is at the moment,' said Kay. 'He was dressed in denim jeans, a dark blue cotton shirt and canvas shoes. The labels in his clothing are common high street and online brands. He wasn't wearing a watch, and there are no other forms of identification such as a wallet or driving licence. He's estimated to be five foot eight – we'll have that clarified after the post mortem because the mummification has caused a degree of shrinkage. His hair is on the long side, as you can see – and for the newcomers, our pathologist clarified it was about that length when he died. Don't believe everything you read in the press about hair growing after death. He wasn't in that cavity long enough, for a start.'

She moved to the second photograph Gavin had provided. 'When we're done, I want you all to have a closer look at his fingertips – Lucas will try to extract prints for us, but they seem worn on his left hand, not so much on the other, which would be unusual for anyone associated with construction work.'

'Maybe he was a guitar player,' said a middle-aged constable from the back of the room.

'Could be,' said Kay. She wrote the suggestion on the board with a question mark under it, then re-capped the pen. 'Parker – can you work with Carys and get the findings she's pulled together to date into HOLMES before tomorrow morning so everyone can access it easily?'

'Yes, guv.' Phillip gave her a thumbs up. 'I've got another couple of computers being installed as well – Theresa in admin managed to rustle them up from somewhere.'

'Good work, thank you.' Kay moved to an enlarged map of the immediate area around the software company's offices. 'Uniform have been working their way around the companies based on the three streets that surround our crime scene, and Andy Grey over at the digital forensics unit has been given copies of the security camera feed from two of the retail shops across the road from the software company. We can't expect much from those to help us given the amount of time that's passed since the renovations were completed, but it's worth a shot.

'CCTV – Barnes, can you coordinate with Hughes and get footage from at least the beginning of June onwards?' Kay added. 'Lucas said our victim dried out very quickly, so we'll work on the basis that he was killed during the heatwave this summer. Let's have a look to see if there was any suspicious activity around the site while works were ongoing, and then the two months afterwards while the premises were empty.'

'Will do.'

'Is it definitely a murder, guv?' said Parker.

'Given the size of the blow to his skull and the angle at which he was struck, we should assume our victim was murdered rather than it being an accident until we have the results from the post mortem. Regardless of how he died, he didn't fall into that cavity. He had help to get in there,' said Kay. She exhaled, dropped the pen to the desk next to her, then cast her eyes over the anxious faces that peered at the whiteboard.

'So, let's find out what happened to him, shall we?'

FIVE

Late the following afternoon Kay elbowed open the door, swearing under her breath as hot coffee slopped out of the takeout cup and over her hand.

She flicked the worst of the liquid away and hurried towards her desk, the noise levels in the open plan space competing with the racket in the street outside from congested traffic and an ambulance fighting to make its way through two lanes of nose-to-tail vehicles.

She'd spent the last four hours at headquarters, first with DCI Sharp bringing the chief superintendent up to date with the start of the investigation and providing an outline of how she planned to manage it before heading back to the town centre station, and then liaising with the media relations team to discuss how to cope with the barrage of enquiries from press and public alike following the previous night's televised media conference.

The sun had long disappeared over the horizon by the time she'd finished and hurried into the incident room to try and catch up with her team before they went home for the night.

She placed the cup on her desk, eyed the flashing light on her desk phone with a glare, then emitted a sigh and began to attack the emails that had multiplied in the hours she'd been at headquarters.

Barnes glanced up from his notebook and raised his eyebrow, his mobile phone to his ear.

Kay shook her head and forced a smile.

The whole day had left her disquieted.

Around her, officers and detectives worked with the frantic buzz that only a new murder investigation could cause, and here she was having to fight her corner with senior management to ensure her team got the resources they needed to deliver the right result.

'Everything all right?' said Barnes, ending his call and tossing his phone onto his desk.

'Yes,' said Kay, and reached out for her computer mouse, wiggling it to waken the screen again. 'The

Chief Super seems happy with the way we've got ourselves set up here, at least.'

Barnes leaned across, lowering his voice conspiratorially. 'I've heard she plays the *Times* Sudoku—'

'Nothing unusual about tha—'

'With a *pen*.'

Kay snatched up the soft stress ball Gavin had left on her desk and pitched it at Barnes, who ducked and then grinned at her.

She laughed, grateful to him for lifting her mood a little. 'Behave. Where are we up to with tasks? Have you managed to shed any light on the construction works over the summer?'

'I'll show you,' said Barnes. He led the way across the room to where the whiteboard stood, now covered in various pinned notes and different coloured marker pen ink. He tapped a photograph of the building that had been taken prior to the redevelopment of the site. 'So, this is what the place used to look like.'

'I'd forgotten what an eyesore it was,' said Kay.

'Ripe for renovation, that's for sure. The bank sold the site at auction – the last tenant left in November the previous year. It was purchased by Hillavon Developments, whose registered offices are in Rochester. The owner, Alexander Hill, lives in Broadstairs.'

'Has anyone spoken to him?' said Kay.

'Gavin's going to follow up later today. Apparently, the bloke plays golf until one o'clock on Tuesdays and keeps his phone switched off until the nineteenth hole. He hasn't returned any of Gavin's calls yet.'

'Tell Gavin to let him know that we can always conduct the interview in one of our rooms here if he's not going to take this matter seriously.'

'Will do, guv.'

'What do we know about him?'

'Hillavon Developments – or Alexander Hill if you like – is an architect by trade, so he designed the new layout for the building and then contracted out the project management and construction to another company, Brancourt and Sons Limited.'

'Where are they based?' said Kay.

'Here in Maidstone. Has been since the 1920s, according to their website,' said Barnes. 'I was planning on contacting them after we speak with the developer in case he tells us something we can question them about.'

'Let's get on with it and speak to someone at Brancourt and Sons as soon as possible. No doubt they're expecting a phone call from us after last night's news was broadcast, and the rumours will be spreading. I'd rather have as much information as possible so we can keep this investigation moving. Who's running the family business these days?'

'John Brancourt,' said Barnes. 'Lives over at Coxheath, and took over from his father thirty years ago. Seems to be a family tradition reading through the history on their website – the business is passed down to the first son in each generation before his thirtieth birthday.'

'Right, get onto John Brancourt and arrange to interview him.' She waited while her colleague made a note, and then continued. 'Going back to the building, who were the last tenants before the place was sold? There was a boutique or something in the retail space below, wasn't there?'

'Yes, where the reception area is now.' Barnes reached out to a neat pile of stapled documents on the table next to Kay and turned the pages, his brow creased until he found what he needed and jabbed the page with his forefinger. 'Here you go. There was a fashion outlet below – Pia always reckoned it was too overpriced for Maidstone, which might have been why it closed a couple of months before the building was put up for sale. On the floor above that, there was a bloodstock licensing agency for racehorses. The top floor was used on a part-time basis by a graphic design company. Carys tracked down those tenants, and uniform will be out taking statements first thing tomorrow.'

'Any issues before the place was sold?' said Kay.

'You mean tenants taking umbrage at being evicted?' Barnes shook his head. 'Not as far as we're aware. Put it this way, there's nothing on the system so unless the interviews that uniform do tomorrow shed any light on something, then no. No issues.'

Kay crossed her arms over her chest as she assessed the information gathered in the first twenty-four hours. 'I don't like this one at all, Ian.'

'Different, isn't it?'

'What on earth was he doing there in the first place? I mean, if there was an accident or something during the redevelopment works then we'd have heard about it. The Health and Safety Executive would have been crawling over that site within hours. You can't cover up something like that, not these days.'

Barnes scratched his chin. 'We're still working up a list of everyone who had access to the site once the renovations began.'

'You're doing a great job, Ian. It's like Sharp

always says, we don't always get the breakthrough we need in the first twenty-four hours – despite what the training manuals tell us.' She gestured across the photographs. 'I mean, this is a good start.'

'Guv, you don't think Gavin has a point?' said Barnes, lowering his voice.

'About what?' Kay peered across at him, and then frowned. 'Oh, wait. The cats? For good luck?'

'Well? What if someone did put him in that cavity on purpose?' He shrugged and looked away, two spots of red appearing on his cheeks.

'Look, let's not rule it out. I think it's unlikely we're looking at a sacrificial killing but let's face it – at the moment, we haven't got anything else as a motive, have we?' Kay turned to face the incident room, a mixture of officers in uniform or business suits creating a blur of activity. 'How did the briefing go?'

'Good. I think everyone knows what they need to do and are keen to get on with it. Parker's finished getting HOLMES up to date so everyone else can start adding their notes as they go now and at least we're able to print out the reports we need. Carys has added the information about the tenants she found as well as the formal data from Companies House, and

Hughes has got two constables helping him go through the CCTV footage we've got to date.'

Kay exhaled, letting out some of the frustration that had been starting to seep into her system during the sojourn at headquarters. 'I knew I could count on you, Ian. Thanks. Get yourself home and hopefully we'll make some headway tomorrow.'

SIX

Kay gathered up the hessian tote bags from the back seat of her car, elbowed the door shut and crossed to the front door of her house, her ears still ringing from the screeching of a toddler at the supermarket checkout minutes before.

The door opened before she could lower the shopping to fish out her keys.

'Evening, detective.'

She smiled. 'Hey, you. Here – take some of these. They weigh a ton.'

Her other half, Adam, obliged by taking two of the bags from her and chuckled as he opened the top of one of them. 'I nearly phoned you to say we need more wine but I see you sorted that as a priority.'

'Yes, I didn't think you'd fancy white in this

weather so I bought you a Rioja and a Pinot Noir,' she said, shutting the door and dropping the security chain into place. 'You choose.'

A rich aroma teased her senses as she followed him into the kitchen, and then she saw what was on the centre worktop and froze.

'Oh no.'

A glass case took up one third of the wide surface, a plastic lid over the top of it peppered with ventilation holes and a thick layer of sawdust and shredded newspaper covering the floor of it.

Adam turned from where he was unpacking the bags next to the refrigerator and raised an eyebrow. 'What's up?'

Kay pointed at the glass case. 'Please tell me the snake's not back here.'

Her veterinary husband laughed.

Two years ago, he had brought home a sick snake whose owners were away on holiday. Having solved an investigation with her close-knit team to arrest and charge a vicious killer, she'd arrived home and discovered that the snake had escaped. Kay had perched on the kitchen worktop until Adam had finally located the reptile behind the washing machine after several minutes of panicked searching.

'No, not a snake. Sid's in fine fettle, you'll be

pleased to know.' Adam scrunched up the empty bags and took the two Kay was holding before placing them on the worktop next to the case and beckoning to her to join him. 'Come and have a look. I think you'll like this.'

She followed him across to the glass case. 'It's the old aquarium from out in the garage isn't it?'

'Yes. It's all I had at short notice – that's why I've used a seed tray as a lid. At least it's got the holes already in it for ventilation, so that saved me a job.'

Kay moved closer to the glass and peered inside.

She noticed that Adam had added a piece of plastic guttering pipe, and had turned it upside down so that it formed a short tunnel at one end of the aquarium. A water bottle had been placed on the glass beside it and next to that, a second bowl of seeds and chopped up vegetables looked as if it had been recently ransacked.

Movement from within the tunnel caught her eye, and then a nose and whiskers appeared moments before a sandy-coloured furry creature shuffled forwards and then rose shakily on its hind legs.

'Aww, it's a gerbil!'

'Told you you'd like him.'

'What's his name?'

'Cornflake.'

'What? Seriously?'

Adam shrugged. 'His owner is eight years old.'

Kay narrowed her eyes as she watched the rodent wobble across the sawdust towards the water bowl. 'What's wrong with him?'

'He had a stroke over the weekend, poor thing,' said Adam. 'Unfortunately, it's quite common amongst these. They make great pets but they don't last much longer than three or four years.'

'How old is Cornflake?'

'Three and a half. Angela – that's Cassie's mum – is a bit squeamish when it comes to giving him his medicine so I offered to look after him for the next week or so. He's making a good recovery so I'm sure he'll be back home with her and Cassie before long.'

'Will he be okay?'

'They're remarkably resilient creatures,' said Adam. 'He'll adapt in time – he'll probably lean to the left like he is now for the rest of his life, but other than that he'll be fine.'

'That's good.' Kay's stomach rumbled and she turned away from the glass case. 'Sorry, but I'm starving. Are you okay to put this lot away while I go and get changed?'

'Go for it. I'll be dishing up in half an hour.'

'Thanks.'

Kay headed upstairs, hanging up her suit jacket before stripping the rest of her clothes from her weary body and stepping into the en suite shower.

As she let the jet of hot water pour over her scalp and scrubbed the day's grime from her skin, her mind turned to the recent anniversary she and Adam had chosen to keep to themselves.

Two years ago, Kay had returned to work after a Professional Standards investigation by Kent Police had left her bereft – and childless.

Only her close team, and her mentor – DCI Devon Sharp – knew the full extent of the personal trauma she and Adam had endured after she had been unfairly targeted.

An ache tore at her chest as the memories resurfaced, her relaxed state releasing the numbed grief she kept to herself. She wiped her eyes, tears lending a salty taste to the water that cascaded over her cheeks and lips, and then turned off the faucet.

After towelling off her skin with a fierceness that left her arms and legs red, Kay released her hair from the top knot she had tied and wiped the condensation from the mirror above the basin.

She scowled at her reflection, pulled the cord to switch off the lights, then moved across the bedroom to a chest of drawers and dragged out a favourite sweatshirt. Pulling on a pair of jeans, she combed her hair.

As she turned to leave the room, her eyes fell upon the plastic bottle of sleeping tablets on her bedside table.

Her heart skipped a beat, and Kay forced down the sense of panic that bubbled at her stomach.

Fear threatened, hard on the heels of the grief that had lowered her resilience.

She had faced death a year ago, fought against an adversary who had wrapped his hands around her throat and tried to extinguish her life.

It was only the quick thinking of DCI Sharp that had saved her from the clutches of Jozef Demiri. She still bore the internal scars from the ordeal to which the organised crime boss had subjected her, and refused to take any prescribed medication for fear of losing her job.

For Adam's sake, she had continued to take the homeopathic remedy on a daily basis but a sense of unbalance gripped her.

It was all she could do not to thrust her hands out to the side as she descended the stairs.

Thirteen steps, but every one of them loaded with guilt.

She hadn't told Adam about the nightmares that had returned since the summer.

She hadn't spoken to Dr Zoe Strathmore following her initial appointment earlier in the year, instead assuring the psychiatrist's receptionist that she was fine; that she was too busy; that her calendar was too full for any follow-up appointment.

For nine months.

A trembling wracked her calves and Kay grasped the bannister, sinking onto the penultimate tread as the spasm enveloped her.

She fought down the sensation, her chest constricting as she drew her knees under her chin, her eyes finding the blinking lights of the security panel to the right of the front door.

It hadn't yet been activated; she or Adam would initiate the sequence before climbing the stairs to bed, but its presence calmed her. There would be no-one breaking into the house tonight.

Kay lowered her forehead to her knees. 'I am not a victim,' she muttered. 'I am *not* a victim. I can do this.'

Movement over her shoulder shook her from her meditation and she launched herself to her feet, ran her fingers through her hair and patted her cheeks.

She felt the colour return to her skin as Adam

emerged from the kitchen, a quizzical expression in his eyes.

'I thought I heard your voice. Everything okay?'

'Yes.' She forced a smile and followed him back into the kitchen.

'I've opened the Pinot.'

'Thanks.' Kay sank onto one of the bar stools at the central kitchen worktop and took a sip from the glass of wine Adam had poured for her. She watched for a moment as Adam returned to the stove and checked the pots steaming on the hob, and then cleared her throat. 'When was the last time you visited Elizabeth?'

Adam froze, the wooden spoon held aloft.

'What?'

Adam balanced the spoon on one of the saucepan handles and then moved across to where she sat. He frowned. 'I've been so busy with the practice over the past few weeks – no, months.'

Kay watched as he bit his lip, his shoulders slumping.

'About ten weeks, I suppose,' he said.

'We don't talk about her anymore. It's like, once Demiri was out of our lives, everything to do with him went as well. Including our daughter.' Kay reached across the worktop and clasped his hand. 'Why?'

He squeezed her fingers, and then walked around to where she sat and enveloped her in a hug before kissing her. 'You've been busy, too. It doesn't mean we don't care.'

'Doesn't it?'

'No, it doesn't.' He sighed, and rubbed her back. 'Life goes on, whether we like it or not. People depend on us.'

'I suppose so.'

'Are you going to tell me what's really bothering you? This isn't just about Elizabeth, is it?'

Kay sniffed, and tried to ignore the stinging sensation at the corners of her eyes.

'Lucy from admin was in the office last week. It's the first time she's been in since she went on maternity leave. She brought her baby, a little boy. Stephen.' She wiped at her cheeks, a shuddering sigh wracking her slight frame. 'She looked so happy.'

'Come here.'

He enveloped her in his arms and kissed the top of her head while she cried into his soft cotton shirt, fighting against the utter wretchedness that engulfed her.

After a few moments, she raised her gaze to his. 'Thank you.'

A faint smile teased his mouth. 'It's a bit shit, isn't it?'

'It is.'

She eased away from his embrace and reached over the worktop to a box of tissues, then dabbed at her eyes and blew her nose.

She turned to see Adam eyeing her warily. 'What is it?'

'Look after yourself, Hunter. I worry about you.'

SEVEN

A blustery wind tugged at Kay's coat the following morning as she followed Barnes from the pool vehicle across a muddy construction yard towards a pockmarked building marked "site office".

A biting chill nipped at her ears, and she cursed under her breath before hurrying over the threshold leaving Barnes to close the door behind them, and then tugged at the scarf at her neck while a bemused-looking woman stared at them from behind a reception desk.

'You should have been here last March,' she said. 'Like flipping Antarctica out there, it was. What can I do for you?'

Kay held up her warrant card. 'DI Kay Hunter and DS Ian Barnes, here to see John Brancourt.'

'Ah, right. No problem. Take a seat – the heater's on over there – and help yourself to tea or coffee from the machine. I'll tell him you're here.'

'Thanks.'

Kay turned to see Barnes already making his way to where a small fan heater had been placed on a rug between two chairs and hurried to join him, holding out her frozen hands to the hot air being blasted through a tiny vent at the top.

The detective sergeant jerked his chin towards the window and a row of construction equipment lined up in the yard outside. 'Obviously spends his money on those rather than the central heating,' he muttered.

Kay smiled. 'Probably why the business is still successful after all these years trading.'

'Detective Hunter?'

She turned around.

Kay estimated the man to be in his late fifties, his stocky frame offset by a shock of light brown hair.

'I'm John Brancourt,' he said, wandering over to where they stood, his hand outstretched.

Kay shook hands and introduced Barnes. 'Thanks for seeing us, Mr Brancourt. Is there somewhere we can talk in private?'

'Of course, come on through to my office.'

Without waiting for an answer, he spun on his

heel and led the way past the bemused gaze of the receptionist and down a narrow unlit corridor.

At the end, he stood to one side to let Kay and Barnes pass before closing the door and gesturing to two chairs next to a cluttered desk.

'Have a seat. Excuse the mess. Sandra out there keeps pestering me to tidy it, but I'm not sure I'd find anything if I did.'

'Thanks,' said Kay, and waited until Barnes had settled and pulled out his notebook. 'I presume you've heard about the body that was discovered in the Petersham Building on Monday morning?'

'I heard something on the radio driving into work yesterday, yes. That's Alexander Hill's building,' said Brancourt, a frown creasing his brow. 'I worked on it over the summer.'

'We're aware of that, Mr Brancourt,' said Kay.

'Call me John. What do you need from me? I'm afraid I don't have the final plans for the building to record what was done – Alex will have to give you those. We're still waiting for him to approve them. These things can take a while.'

'Actually, we were hoping you could tell us anything you might know about how that body might have got there in the first place,' said Kay. 'I have to insist that anything we discuss here isn't mentioned to the media, but we're trying to find out who the victim is.'

'Haven't you identified him?' said Brancourt.

'We can't say much about the case or the victim at the present time,' said Barnes. 'Not until the post mortem examination has been concluded. We wondered whether you were aware of anyone who had been threatened during the construction phase – particularly before the carpet fitters began work?'

'Nothing I can think of, no.'

'How long have you run the family business, Mr Brancourt?' said Kay.

He brushed an imaginary piece of lint from the breast pocket of his shirt, the movement drawing attention to the embroidered logo across it, and then set his shoulders.

'I started working here with my father when I was old enough to walk,' he said. 'Started my apprenticeship in the yard out there when I was fourteen, worked all hours and in all weather conditions until my father called me into a meeting on my twenty-first birthday.'

'You've been running it ever since?' said Barnes.

Brancourt shook his head, a smile creasing his features. 'No, I had to wait another six years until he thought I was capable of that, but it was enough to know I'd impressed him and that he'd be passing it down to me like his father before him. Even when he retired when I was twenty-nine, he kept working for the business in a part-time capacity. He knew what reputation was worth, and he was determined I'd be as successful as he'd been. Both my grandfather and great-grandfather took over the running of the business before they were thirty, so it's a running tradition. My son, Damien, will do the same before his thirtieth birthday.'

'And, have you been successful?'

'We've had our fair share of ups and downs, I'll admit,' said Brancourt. He sighed. 'It was hard ten years ago, and like a lot of businesses we struggled and had to lay off some of our workers. But we kept the apprentices, and we kept the men who had been with us since my father's time – I wasn't so short-sighted to lose the key people I'd need to run this business when work picked up again and, sure enough, we turned things around.'

'Any financial issues during that time?' said Kay, and then held up her hand as Brancourt opened his mouth to protest, and rephrased her question. 'Would anyone have any reason to hold a grudge against you or your company? Or your employees for that matter?'

The construction manager sat back in his chair and drummed his fingers on the desk for a moment before speaking.

'I can't think of anyone, no. We were very lucky when we did have that quiet spell because we were able to pay off all the contractors we had working for us. We only kept the full-time employees, like I said. And with all the contractors, we assured them we'd be in touch as soon as work became available. They were all good people and many did come back here if they hadn't found jobs elsewhere. I'm always very careful not to sully my reputation in this business. Everybody knows everybody.'

'Did you hear any rumours on site, any indication that there might have been a disagreement between other contractors involved in the works?' said Barnes.

'If there was, it was kept away from me,' said John. 'I attended a site meeting every week once work got underway, which is routine practice. If there were specific items that needed addressing then I went there to oversee things to make sure it went smoothly, but no – I never heard anyone talking about any other issues. It was just the usual day-to-day stuff that comes with running a redevelopment project like that.'

Kay caught Barnes's attention and then rose from

her seat and held out her business card. 'All right, Mr Brancourt. Thank you for your time. If you do think of anything that could help us with our investigation, please phone me.'

'Let me see you out.'

He gestured for Barnes to lead the way back along the corridor to the reception area, then shook their hands and followed them to the door.

Kay turned to see John Brancourt appraising the busy yard before his eyes met hers.

'You understand, Detective Hunter,' he said. 'It's all about reputation. Without it, we're nothing.'

EIGHT

That afternoon, Carys and Gavin stood at the perimeter of a council-run car park and squinted against the horizontal rain towards their target, a nondescript two-storey building on the opposite side of the A2.

Even from her position, Carys could see the brass plaque that labelled the office as belonging to Alexander Hill, member of the Architects Registration Board and whatever letters followed after that.

'Tell me why you couldn't just phone him again,' she said as she battled with a flimsy umbrella that was determined to turn inside out for the third time.

'Because he doesn't answer his phone and I'm sick of leaving messages.'

'Not playing golf in this weather, was he?'

'God knows, but his receptionist told me that he's in the office until four o'clock today so I thought it'd be a good idea to pay him a visit and bring to his attention we're dealing with a dead man at one of his properties.'

Satisfied that she'd have a modicum of protection from the elements, Carys led the way across the busy road, negotiating a puddle she suspected disguised a deep pothole with a quick side-step, and then stood on the pavement outside Hill's property development business.

'Okay if I lead this one?' she said.

Her colleague frowned. 'Why?'

'Because he's ignoring you. So, I'm thinking he's got something to hide. You can push him, I'll charm him. Sound good?'

Gavin's shoulders relaxed. 'Okay, yeah. That makes sense.'

'Don't worry, I'm not going to steal your thunder if he's guilty of something.'

She grinned, then turned and pushed the door open before he had a chance to respond, dropped her umbrella into a stand by a strategically placed doormat, and then moved towards the reception desk.

'Afternoon.' She jerked her thumb over her

shoulder, before holding out her warrant card. 'My colleague here spoke to you earlier, I believe?'

'Oh, yes. Yes, he did.' The receptionist's eyes widened, and she put aside the book she'd been reading. 'Can I help?'

'We'd like to speak to Alexander Hill, please.'

'He's busy, but I can—'

'Now, please.' Carys smiled. 'DC Piper has left several messages over the course of the past forty-eight hours, but your boss seems to think his golf handicap is more important than a murder investigation. If he'd like to accompany us back to Maidstone police station to attend a formal interview instead, that's fine, but—'

'I'll get him for you.'

The receptionist pushed her chair back and hurried towards a door behind her desk, pulling it closed behind her.

Carys turned to find Gavin shaking his head at her.

'You're something else, Miles.'

'It worked, didn't it?'

'You're supposed to be the one playing nice, remember?'

Approaching footsteps prevented any retort from

Carys as the receptionist pushed through the door moments before her boss.

Alexander Hill peered through bifocal glasses at his intruders, sniffed, then beckoned to the two detectives. 'I suppose if you're here you might as well come through.'

Carys hurried after him, catching the door as it swung shut behind the property developer who set a brisk pace along an uneven corridor and up a narrow flight of stairs.

The treads creaked under Hill's footsteps, his large frame blocking the light from an upstairs window and creating a shadow over the carpet under her feet.

She raised her gaze as she followed him, wondering whether tweed was actually still in fashion, and noting the way he wore his hair in a spiky manner similar to the colleague who traipsed behind her.

The man was a motley collection of contradictions.

Hill paused at a doorway at the top of the landing and gestured for them to go through, before moving to a chair behind a desk covered in receipts and spreadsheets.

'My apologies, detectives. You find me at a

stressful time – my book-keeper left us last week due to poor health and I'm trying to get my head around this year's accounts before the tax year ends.'

Gavin helped himself to the chair on the left, reaching into his jacket pocket for his notebook, and said nothing. He glared at Hill.

Carys remained passive as the property developer straightened his tie and sank into his own chair.

If the man felt uncomfortable, she didn't care. She wanted answers.

'Why haven't you returned my colleague's phone calls and messages, Mr Hill?'

In response, he gestured to the paperwork strewn across his desk, but Gavin spoke before he could reply.

'Paperwork isn't a valid excuse, Mr Hill. Nor is playing golf. We're dealing with what appears to be the brutal murder of a man whose body was found encased within a building you developed over the course of last summer. And we'd like some answers, please.'

Chastened, Hill rested his arms on the desk and appeared to look contrite. 'I'm very sorry, Detective Piper. I realise I should've returned your calls, and I apologise. What is it you'd like to ask me?'

'Why did you decide to award the construction

management of the redevelopment works to Brancourt and Sons?'

'John and his team had worked on similar contracts for me over the past three years – smaller scopes of work than the Petersham Building, but always to a high degree of finishing. It's the older companies like his that can be counted on; the ones who've been established a long time. When I sent out the tender, I knew his would come back the strongest. He wasn't the cheapest, but I knew what to expect.'

'A known quantity, you mean?'

'Exactly, and that's often hard to find in this industry.'

'What happened after you awarded the contract to Brancourt and Sons?' said Gavin. 'Did you relinquish all control over the project?'

'Not at all. John's remit was to take care of the day-to-day running of the redevelopment work – awarding contracts for work such as lighting, telecommunications, carpentry, et cetera and making sure it was all completed in line with the project schedule. Basically, the purpose of his contract was to save me managing the paperwork – and to spread the risk so my company wasn't wholly responsible financially for getting the place finished on time.'

'Brancourt mentioned he was waiting for copies

of the finished plans for the completed redevelopment works from you,' said Gavin. 'Any idea when those will be made available?'

'I'm sorry, I'm not sure at the moment. My document controller works part-time and we're still trying to catch up with all the work we completed over the summer. I can have a set of drawings issued to you as soon as they're ready if you like?'

'That would be appreciated, thank you.'

'Do you recall any issues during the works?' said Carys. 'Any altercations between contractors that might've led to this man's death?'

Hill shook his head. 'Nothing was brought to my attention when I attended site meetings. That's the usual forum for contractors to air any grievances, so it can be minuted and then sorted out.'

'Have you spoken to the media at all about this?' said Carys.

Hill shook his head. 'It's why I've been avoiding answering the phone to be honest. Gilly out there has been fielding calls to this office but I haven't dared check my voicemail messages since the news broke.' He held up his mobile. 'I haven't switched this on since Tuesday.'

'What are you afraid of, Mr Hill?' said Gavin.

'Afraid?'

'A man in your circumstances, running your own business, expected to be on call for any number of queries from your clients and contractors, not answering his phone? That doesn't seem likely,' said Gavin.

Hill tugged at his earlobe, but said nothing.

'Is someone threatening you?' said Carys. She reached out and placed her hand on the paperwork. 'You can tell us, if that's the case.'

'Not threatening me, no. But there were some – indiscretions – regarding the contracts at the Petersham Building I wasn't happy with. I wondered…' He removed his glasses and polished a lens with the corner of his shirt before replacing them. 'I wondered if that had something to do with all this.'

'In what way?' said Gavin. 'Weren't you responsible for managing the contracts?'

'Only the high level ones. Like I said, the construction management team, Brancourt and Sons, were engaged to run all the on-site contracts. My role in these things is to locate suitable premises to develop, raise the capital and then manage the main contractor – Brancourt and Sons in the case of the Petersham Building.'

'What sort of indiscretions do you mean?' said Carys.

Hill reached out and tidied a stack of pages on the corner of his desk, then sighed. 'Look, you didn't hear this from me all right? I don't need the trouble.'

Carys remained silent, thankful her colleague did the same.

After a moment, Hill took the hint and held up his hands. 'There have been rumours going around that Mark Sutton's company isn't exactly legitimate.'

'Who is Mark Sutton?' said Gavin.

'He owns Sutton Site Security. Brancourt and Sons awarded them the contract to maintain a fenced perimeter around the building while the works were ongoing to make sure there were no attempted break-ins. Some of the contractors left valuable equipment there rather than take it away each afternoon, and then of course there were the supplies being stored there prior to installation.'

'In what way is Mark Sutton's business not legitimate?' said Carys.

'Have you met him?'

'No.'

'He's got a reputation for being a bit of a crook, and he surrounds himself with people who have a similar background to his.'

'Of the criminal variety?' said Carys.

Hill shrugged. 'I couldn't say. Like I said, I don't

need the trouble and Sutton isn't someone I'd want to deal with, which made John's selection of his company awkward to say the least. I really don't need that sort of negative publicity on top of everything else that's happened this week.'

Carys signalled to Gavin, then turned back to Hill and slid one of her business cards across the cluttered desk towards him.

'We'll see ourselves out, but we'll need to talk to you again during the course of our enquiries. In the meantime, if you think of anything else that will help us, you can reach me on that number. Or, you can phone DC Piper. After all, you have his number in your phone, right?'

Hill nodded, a sheepish expression crossing his features. 'I do, yes.'

Carys said nothing further until they'd retreated to the reception area and she'd retrieved her umbrella.

Once outside, she turned to Gavin.

'Callous bastard, isn't he? All he could think about was the potential damage to his business, not the fact someone died at the site of one of his projects.'

'Makes you wonder why,' said Gavin.

NINE

Kay wrapped her fingers around the warm ceramic of her coffee cup and assessed the investigative officers and administrative staff who were hurrying to join her at the far end of the incident room.

As she waited for them to find seats, she paced in front of the whiteboard mulling over the morning's interview with John Brancourt, and then glanced up at movement by the door.

She smiled as Detective Chief Inspector Devon Sharp raised his hand in greeting before pushing his way between the desks and the assembled throng.

'Mind if I join you for this one?' he said as he reached her. 'I thought it'd save you coming over to headquarters later this afternoon to give the Chief

Super an update. I can report back to her and let you get on.'

'You're a lifesaver, guv – thanks. What's the latest from the media liaison unit?'

'The vultures are circling,' he said. 'Slow news week.'

'Dammit, that's a shame.'

'I know.'

In Kay's experience, if a murder caught the media's attention during a week when there were no major events or other incidents to report upon, the ensuing investigation would become their sole focus. The effect was one of constant interruption as phone calls, emails and even personal visits by hopeful journalists cajoling for a story ahead of their competitors intensified.

'There's a news crew outside at the moment,' said Sharp.

'What, here?'

'They've had the sense to set up at the bottom of Gabriel's Hill, but you might want to warn your lot. And if any of you are ambushed outside by the press, I want to know about it immediately, all right?'

'No problem. Thanks for the heads up.'

He nodded, then glanced over his shoulder. 'Well,

it looks like everyone's here. Don't mind me. I'll grab a coffee and listen in.'

'Thanks. There are digestive biscuits on my desk.'

He grinned before turning away, and Kay took a sip of her own hot drink before setting the cup down on the desk next to her.

She rarely saw her friend and mentor at the Maidstone police station now that Devon Sharp had been promoted to the role of Detective Chief Inspector, despite his best attempts to stay away from the Kent Police headquarters on Sutton Road. She missed the easy banter that had accompanied the previous investigations that they'd worked on together in the past but accepted that it was the natural course of promotion and responsibility.

At least they managed to catch up every few weeks for dinner with their respective partners to socialise.

'Gav, tell me you managed to speak with Alexander Hill this morning?' she said as the younger detective took a seat close to the whiteboard.

'Yes, me and Carys went over to Rochester earlier,' he said, and ran through his notes from the interview. 'Hill stated that he wasn't aware of any issues at site with regard to contractors having disagreements, but he did raise concerns about the site security firm that Brancourt and Sons employed. He told us he thought the owner, Mark Sutton, may have criminal connections.'

Kay stopped writing on the board and raised an eyebrow. 'Oh, yes? Did he say why he thought that?'

'Apparently, Sutton has a reputation for being a crook and may even be employing people of a criminal nature.' Gavin indicated to his colleague. 'We were going to have a dig around to see what we could find out.'

'Good. Let me know what you put together over the next twenty-four hours.' Kay scratched another note on the whiteboard, then brushed a wisp of hair from her face and turned to her colleagues. 'Do a complete review of Sutton's business – carefully, mind, so we don't alert him to the fact until we're ready to speak to him.'

'Guv.'

'Carys – have all the previous tenants been interviewed by uniform?'

'Yes, guv.' The detective constable rose from her seat and cleared her throat before addressing her colleagues, quoting from her notebook. 'Nothing very much stands out from my review of the statements, I'm afraid. The owner of the boutique, a Mrs Felicity Hawkins, says she ended her tenancy three months before works commenced so she didn't experience any problems from contractors. She said her trade took a nosedive once everyone heard about the redevelopment – apparently she had customers telling her they wouldn't buy clothes in case they couldn't return them if they didn't fit, things like that.'

'Fickle,' said Kay, 'but that's human nature, I suppose. Who else have you got?'

Carys ran her gaze over her notes. 'The owner of the bloodstock licensing agency retired – he lives in Berkshire now, and similarly stated that he had no issues when renting his office space and wasn't even aware that the works had finished. Finally, the tenants who were on the top floor run a graphic design agency. It's a husband and wife team – Peter and Jane Wilberforce. Uniform spoke to Peter who told them they were relieved the tenancy had ended earlier because they'd been struggling to find new clients. They've been running their business from home since the works began.'

'None of them sound like the sort to hold a grudge,' said Barnes.

'True,' said Kay. 'All right, for now we'll put the tenants to one side. They're not under suspicion per se, unless something else crops up during the course of our enquiries.'

She wrote a cross next to each of the tenants' names on the whiteboard and then re-capped the pen and turned to the team. 'Who spoke to the carpet fitters?'

Sergeant Hughes raised his hand. 'Me, guv. There were two of them tasked with doing the upstairs offices – Michael Blake and Andy James. I spoke to Michael first. He said that he didn't notice anything unusual while they were working in the building – he was quite shocked when I told him what had happened. He said the underlay was fitted first, then they spent a day working in one of the offices at the rear of the building. When they went back to work in the front office two days later, he said nothing looked like it had been disturbed. Andy James's statement was the same – no unusual activity spotted.'

'No blood stains on the floor or underlay?' said Kay. 'No signs of a struggle?'

'Nothing, guv – no.'

'Maybe the damage to our victim's skull was caused when he was crammed into the cavity?' said Barnes. 'We've only assumed he was clobbered over the head and killed.'

'Good point,' said Kay. She wrote Barnes's suggestion on the whiteboard, then reviewed the notes to date. Satisfied she'd caught everything, she turned back to her team.

'Mark Sutton and his site security business are now key elements to this enquiry, and I want all of you to support Gavin and Carys with that lead. I want a full update first thing tomorrow morning, is that clear?'

She nodded at the rumble of agreement, and then dismissed them before turning back to the whiteboard.

Somehow, she would see that their victim found justice.

TEN

Kay pushed the duvet away from her face, rolled over and reached out blindly for her watch on the bedside table.

Her fingers eventually found the stainless steel surface of the wristband and she tugged it closer, blinking through bleary eyes at the illuminated dials.

Three forty-five.

She dropped the watch back onto the polished wooden surface and wondered whether she should turn on the bedside light.

If she did, she knew she'd never get back to sleep. It would be too tempting to pad across the carpet to the dressing table where her phone was on charge, and then she'd spend the next hour checking emails before deciding it was too late to fight her insomnia.

Instead, she turned on her back and rested her head on the soft cotton pillowcase, the faint scent of freshly washed linen lending some peace to her frayed nerves.

Adam snored softly, his back to her and the duvet rising up to his calves. He hated his feet being covered no matter the season, and she envied his knack of falling asleep the moment the light was out.

She knew it was because he never knew when he might get a call-out during the night hours – he simply tried to get as much sleep as possible.

Her thoughts returned to her sudden awakening, and she strained her ears.

Something had wrested her from her sleep, that was for sure.

She couldn't recollect any nightmares – no memories of her near-death experience at the hands of one of Kent's most evil killers resonated in her sleep-deprived mind.

No, it was something else.

Something close.

She held her breath as the sound of a car in the lane reached her ears, the engine muffled by the new double-glazed windows they'd had installed eighteen months ago.

It hadn't been cheap, but they'd insisted on locks

being fitted to all the frames – a testament to a previous break-in that had fractured Kay's confidence in the sanctuary of her own home.

Still, she strained her hearing to try to work out the vehicle's movements as it drew closer and then accelerated past their driveway and up to the roundabout that separated the old houses from the newer housing estate.

Kay exhaled, feeling a little of the tension leaving her body, but a sense of foreboding remained.

It hadn't been the car that had woken her, so what had it been?

Adam snuffled in his sleep, his foot kicking out.

Kay smiled – he'd taken up five-a-side football one evening a week after work and had become obsessed with the sport. No doubt right now he was dreaming about the goal that got away.

A clatter from downstairs sent her heart racing, and she pushed back the duvet, her feet finding the carpet before she launched herself at her mobile phone.

'What's going on?'

Muted streetlight through the curtains silhouetted Adam's form as he raised himself from the bed, his voice confused.

'There's someone downstairs.'

He was awake in an instant. 'Are you sure? We set the alarm.'

'Alarms can be broken,' hissed Kay. 'I'm going down there.'

'Wait.' Adam kicked off the duvet and reached for the pair of trousers he'd thrown over the chair under the window. 'You're not going down there on your own.'

Kay pulled on her jeans and tried not to pace.

The floorboards in the old cottage had a tendency to creak and she had every intention of catching the intruder, rather than give them an early warning that they'd been heard.

'Ready?'

Adam joined her at the bedroom door. 'I'm going first.'

Kay opened her mouth to protest but he'd already ripped the door from its frame and was sprinting along the landing towards the top of the stairs.

As she followed, she spotted the tell-tale flashing green light of the alarm panel next to the front door and confusion swept through her.

Why hadn't the alarm worked?

Adam snatched an umbrella from a tall vase at the foot of the stairs and turned towards the living room. He held up his hand. 'Slowly.'

He shoved the door open with his elbow, and then used his hand to flip the light switch.

The living room was empty, undisturbed.

'Kitchen,' said Kay.

She didn't wait for him, and instead rushed towards the door, anger driving her forwards.

How dare they? After everything she and Adam had been through the past two years – how dare anyone invade the sanctuary they'd worked so hard to recreate. How—

She blinked as the spotlights in the kitchen ceiling sprang to life, skidding to a standstill on the tiled floor.

'Oh my God.'

Adam barrelled into her, her sudden loss in forward momentum catching him by surprise, and then he began to laugh.

'It's not funny.'

Kay walked towards the worktop to where Cornflake's glass enclosure sat, the plastic seed tray Adam had placed on top of it as a makeshift lid now upside down on the floor.

She looked inside, her gaze taking in the mixture of sawdust and gnawed cardboard that the gerbil had corralled into a nest in one corner opposite his food bowl and water bottle, and then turned to Adam.

'Where is he?'

'He must've head-butted the lid off,' he said.

'Is that what I heard?'

'Well it probably took him a few times to make it work.'

'Bloody hell.' Kay searched the floor, terrified that she'd step on the small rodent. 'Where's he gone?'

Adam lurched for the door, closing it before turning back to her. 'Well, he's in here somewhere. I guess we just have to find him.'

Kay glanced at the clock on the oven and groaned as Adam dropped to his hands and knees and began to peer under the cupboards.

'It's four o'clock in the morning. Fat chance of getting back to sleep now.'

ELEVEN

Later that morning, Kay rubbed at tired eyes and tried to focus on Gavin's review of Mark Sutton's business activities, while Barnes accelerated past a moped rider and tapped his fingers on the steering wheel to a tune he whistled under his breath.

Adam had finally coaxed Cornflake from a gap under the refrigerator with a piece of cucumber, then placed the rodent back in its enclosure. He'd secured the lid with half a brick he'd found in the garden before racing out of the door to his first appointment at six o'clock.

Now Sandra, John Brancourt's receptionist, showed Kay and Barnes through to the project manager's office, closing the door behind them.

Kay didn't waste time with niceties as her colleague took a seat beside her.

'Tell us about Sutton Site Security, Mr Brancourt.'

He exhaled. 'I didn't have a lot of choice when it came to them.'

'Oh? In what way?'

'It was less trouble to give them the work than not.'

'Best let us decide that,' said Barnes. 'Go on. What sort of trouble?'

Brancourt pushed his chair back and moved to the window, peering through the blinds at the activity outside before he turned back to them, his face pale. 'You have to be careful how you use this information. I have a family; employees to look after.'

'We'll do what we can,' said Kay. 'What can you tell us?'

'We started issuing tenders out to suppliers for the security works last January,' he said. 'We weren't due to be on site until April but by the time you get enough time to assess the bids and negotiate a contract... well, let's just say it can take a while. We went out to three companies – the minimum required by Hillavon Developments for each contract after doing a risk assessment of the available contractors.

Two days after the tender was released, I got a phone call.'

Kay frowned as a shiver ran across the man's shoulders. 'From whom?'

'I don't know. I-I mean, I could hazard a guess but I'd rather not,' said Brancourt.

'What did the caller say?' said Barnes.

'He said that if I didn't give the work to Sutton Site Security then I'd regret it. That was all. It shook me up, but I've been threatened before – it sort of comes with the territory to be honest.'

'And who do you think made the call?' said Kay.

Brancourt shoved his hands in his jeans pockets and contemplated the carpet tiles for a moment. 'Mark Sutton, the owner. After all, why would a complete stranger tell me to use them? He sounded different though, as if he was trying to disguise his voice so I can't be sure, all right?'

Kay caught the note of panic in his voice and waved him back to his seat. 'We were going to speak to Mark Sutton anyway, given the circumstances of the victim's death, Mr Brancourt.'

He sank into the leather office chair with a sigh. 'Please don't get me wrong, if I can help in any way then I will. But I've got a family to think about; I won't put them in harm's way.'

'Back to the phone call,' said Barnes. 'I take it you ignored the warning?'

Brancourt nodded. 'Yes, until two of our generators disappeared from the yard out there three days later. Two days after that, one of our tool sheds was broken into and half the equipment taken.'

'Did you report it to the police?' said Kay.

Brancourt choked out a laugh. 'Of course I bloody didn't. It was pretty obvious what was going on. A week after the first call, I got another. The bloke on the other end – Sutton or whoever – said that he'd heard I had a security issue, and that perhaps I might want to reconsider his advice. It didn't help that the security company we use here was also one of the tenderers we were waiting to hear back from – it made them look incompetent, especially when we discovered they'd been cutting corners on attendance. Two of the CCTV cameras were faulty, too.'

'What did you do?'

'I told the caller I'd see what I could do.' Brancourt's face reddened. 'In the end, I told our contracts manager to invite Sutton Site Security on top of the three tenderers we'd already gone out to. The tender opening date wasn't for another couple of days and given what had happened here, he probably thought I wanted an alternative to the company we use.'

'But surely you still had to convince everyone once the tenders were in that Sutton Site Security were the company that should be awarded the contract, right? I mean, any of the others could've beaten them on price or experience,' said Kay.

'Oh, they're experienced,' said Brancourt. 'As for the price, well, given that they received the tender after everyone else I left it until late one afternoon to release a tender addendum extending the closing date by forty-eight hours to the other three parties. Of course, by then I had two of the tenders in already. They're sent via email and then the hard copies are dropped into the tender box at reception – that way, we can issue out the opened tenders to the evaluation team quickly. Saves on paper and printing costs.'

'And that gave you the perfect excuse to open up the emails and check the pricing,' said Barnes, his eyes narrowing. 'So you then told Sutton Site Security what to bid at, right?'

Brancourt leaned forward, placing his shaking hands on the desk. 'I didn't have a choice.'

'We'll need copies of their bid and any correspondence in relation to the bid.'

'I-I'm sorry. I can't do that.'

'Why not?'

'Our computer system developed a critical error back in July – the software engineer we brought in to fix it said he reckoned the summer's heatwave was too much for the ventilation system in our server room. By the time we got in on the Monday we'd lost six months' worth of data, including the tender documentation for the site security contract.'

'You're joking,' said Barnes.

The construction manager shook his head, colour rising in his cheeks.

'What about the hard copy documentation?' said Kay, aware of the note of desperation that tinged her words.

'I'm sorry – we don't keep it.' Brancourt shrugged. 'There's no need for it once the bids are opened. Everything's done electronically these days. It's really just a formality.'

'Did anyone query why you favoured Mark Sutton's company?'

'No. And the bid we received supported the tender criteria, so as far as anyone else around here is concerned, they were the right contractor for the job.'

'Wow.' Kay glanced at Barnes, who wore a perplexed expression.

'Why doesn't anyone report them?' he said. 'After all, it's extortion what they did to you.'

Brancourt shrugged. 'Because they're good. Besides, once they were on site, it guaranteed that no other criminals were going to target the project or my company, didn't it?'

TWELVE

Kay elected to take Barnes with her to interview Mark Sutton the next day given the older detective's experience

As she reversed the car into a space near the industrial complex, the detective sergeant glanced up from his mobile phone.

'This says it should be that small unit over there to the left,' he said. 'The one on the end.'

Kay peered across to where he indicated and saw a squat beige-painted line of four business premises, all identical except for the signage above the doors indicating the companies inside.

Each unit had a roll-up door, one of which was open while two employees wrested a large desk from a rental truck and into the building.

'What do you know about the businesses next door?' she said. 'That one looks like it's some sort of furniture reclamation place.'

'Yeah – their website says they sell bric-à-brac and stuff to bars and restaurants,' said Barnes. 'Next to them is a printer cartridge distributor, then you've got a dry-cleaning business between them and Sutton Site Security.'

'Okay. Can you arrange to speak with those businesses once we're done here? Get uniform onto it if you need to, but find out if they've noticed any unusual activity.'

'Will do.'

Kay tugged the keys from the ignition. 'Let's go.'

Barnes zipped up his jacket and hurried after her, his hands shoved into his pockets while he hunkered down against the cold drizzle that peppered the car park. 'I'm presuming you don't have an appointment?'

'You presume correctly,' said Kay. She reached the side of the industrial units and tried to shelter under the shallow gables, then gave up and dashed for the front door of the unit housing Sutton Site Security.

The door opened into a sparse reception area, and a man who Kay estimated to be in his mid-twenties glanced up from his mobile phone with an expression of derision.

'Police?'

Kay held up her warrant card in response. 'I need a word with your boss, Mark Sutton. I'm presuming the new sports car out there is his not yours, and that he's here?'

The receptionist scowled, then jutted his chin at two threadbare chairs that had been placed under a health and safety poster on the far wall. 'Sit down. I'll tell him you're here. What's it about?'

Kay smiled. 'None of your business.'

Barnes waited until the receptionist had stomped off through a door behind the desk, and then turned to Kay.

'Friendly,' he said.

'Hmm.' Kay turned away from the small camera she'd spotted in the ceiling and lowered her voice. 'Keep your eyes and ears open, Ian. Whatever Sutton is up to, it's not going to be all legal. I can tell.'

'Will do.'

His gaze moved to a space over her shoulder, and Kay turned to see a large man with close-shaven black hair bearing down upon them.

He held out his hand, his mouth breaking into a smile that didn't reach his blue eyes.

'Detective Inspector Hunter. I'm Mark Sutton. To what do we owe the pleasure?'

Kay kept her hands in the pockets of her jacket. 'We have some questions in relation to the site security services you provided for the construction works at the Petersham Building. Do you have somewhere we can talk in private?'

He shrugged, the gesture sending a ripple across his broad shoulders before he motioned towards a door to the side of the reception desk. 'We don't use the garage for much. We can talk in there. Hope you don't want coffee. We ran out.'

Sutton pulled a cord to the right of the door and a line of fluorescent lights flickered to life in the ceiling of the large space.

Kay took a moment to get her bearings and worked out that the offices took up half of the unit and had then been extended to create a mezzanine level.

Windows provided the occupants of the office above with a view over the garage, but the room seemed deserted for now. As was the garaging space, save for a row of boxes against one wall and a forklift truck parked amongst the shadows of the back wall.

'Where are all your staff, Mr Sutton?'

'Out working,' he said. 'That's what they get paid for.'

'Seems extravagant to have all this space and leave it empty.'

'Are you telling me how to run my business?'

'Just an observation,' said Kay. 'Tell me how you won the contract to provide site security at the Petersham Building.'

'We met all the tender criteria and beat our competitors' pricing.'

Kay moved towards the boxes.

'What are you doing?' Mark Sutton started after her, but Barnes stepped into his path and the man glared at him.

Barnes stood his ground. The security company owner may have been built like a rugby forward, but Barnes's height gave him some advantage. He held the man's gaze and remained still.

Kay reached the boxes and ran her hand over one of them before glancing over her shoulder.

'What's in these?'

'Stationery supplies.' Sutton side-stepped around Barnes, but didn't move closer. 'We took delivery of them yesterday. Timesheets and stuff.'

Kay moved away, unconvinced but unable to search further without having probable cause to do so.

She was aware Sutton knew she was testing him, and changed tack once more.

'We heard a rumour that you have a habit of intimidating people to ensure you win work,' she said.

'Lies,' said Sutton. He held his hands up in a "what can you do" gesture. 'Our competitors don't like us winning the work. Our clients, however, tend to come back time after time.'

'Do you steal equipment to coerce your clients into employing you?'

He chuckled. 'No, detective, I don't. That would be illegal. Besides, where would I put the stuff? You can see that we're only a small operation.'

Kay looked over his shoulder as the door from the reception area opened and a man's figure appeared silhouetted against the brighter lights beyond.

'Boss, there's an urgent phone call for you,' he said.

Barnes turned at the voice and then back to Kay, his expression incredulous.

She gave a slight shake of her head to silence any words he was thinking of uttering, but shared his surprise.

'Mr Sutton, I didn't know you knew Gary Hudson. Hudson – when did they let you out? I thought your activities with Demiri put you away for a long time.'

The man moved into view, a snarl on his lips. 'Got let out early for good behaviour, no thanks to you.'

Kay turned back to his boss. 'I wouldn't think it'd be good for business to employ a known criminal, Sutton. Unless some of his traits were of use to you?'

He spread his hands. 'My wife always said I was a softie for a stray dog.'

'She must be very understanding.'

'She was, God bless her soul.' Sutton placed his hand over his heart as a benevolent smile crossed his lips. 'Passed away three years ago.'

'Any idea how a dead man came to be in the ceiling cavity of the breakout area in the Petersham Building?'

'What? No,' he said. 'Our scope of work was to provide outside security along the perimeter of the works, detective. No-one went inside unless invited. Not from my company, anyway.'

'Are you aware of anyone else who may have had access, particularly once the flooring contractors had finished and before the carpet fitters were on site?'

'All the records we had to keep in relation to site access were passed to John Brancourt and Alexander

Hill on a daily basis,' said Sutton. 'I have no need to keep them. That documentation formed part of the quality system requirements we had to fulfil. Which we did. You should speak to them. Although, I'm guessing you already have, given that you're here.'

Kay said nothing, and indicated to Barnes that they were leaving before handing a card to Sutton. 'Call me if you recall anything suspicious taking place on site.'

He led them to the door, passing Hudson who aimed a poisonous glare at Kay, and then opened the front door for her.

She let Barnes go ahead of her before turning to Sutton. 'I think you know a lot more about my victim than you're letting on, Mark.'

He sneered, his knuckles turning white as he grasped the door frame.

'Prove it,' he said, and slammed the door in her face.

THIRTEEN

By the time Kay called her team to attention for the afternoon briefing, the energy levels in the room had gained momentum.

As more information came to light and new leads were followed up, the investigation had begun to flourish, the previous sense of inertia leaving the tight-knit group of detectives.

'Let's make a start, everyone,' she called. 'We're going to be in here over the weekend, so the sooner we get this briefing concluded, the sooner you can get home to your families tonight.'

A flurry of activity followed as uniformed officers joined the detectives and civilian staff next to the whiteboard and grabbed whatever chair was closest, perched on the corners of desks or simply leaned against the nearest wall.

Eventually the cacophony died down, and Kay ran through the tasks that had been completed by each senior officer and their teams. One by one, leads were closed out or a decision was made to pursue it further until Kay turned back to the team and cleared her throat.

'When we interviewed John Brancourt, he told us he was still waiting for the final approved construction plans from Alexander Hill that record all the work completed on site. What did he have to say about that when you spoke to him yesterday?'

'It doesn't sound like anything untoward, guv,' said Carys. 'Hill confirmed that Brancourt and Sons will receive the plans, but at the moment they're going through a final approval process and his document controller only works three days a week. With all the redevelopment work he's been involved with, they've got a backlog of something like nine weeks. Those as built plans won't be finalised until the end of March.' She jerked her chin at the paperwork littering Debbie's desk. 'We did get printouts of the plans from the original council building approvals process, though, and those will get logged in over the weekend.'

'I had a quick look at them earlier, guv,' said Gavin, 'but there's nothing unusual marked on them in relation to the kitchen and break area or the office above it.'

'Okay, thanks,' said Kay, fighting to keep the disappointment from her voice.

'How did you get on with the boss of Sutton Site Security?' said Carys.

'He's definitely a person of interest,' said Kay. 'He answered all our questions a little too smoothly for my liking, as if he's spent the past six months rehearsing his responses. I know the discovery of our victim has been all over the news this week, but it felt like Mark Sutton was ready for us. Then there's the fact that Gary Hudson is working for him since being released from prison. And the bloke who was the receptionist – Wayne Markham. Have you come across him before?'

'Can't say the name rings a bell,' said Gavin. 'Got a photo?'

Kay reached into a folder on the desk next to her, and then pinned up a colour image she'd printed off moments before. 'I managed to get a shot while Barnes was pulling out of the car park. It's a bit out of focus. I checked HOLMES, too. He doesn't have a record, and we've never interviewed him before.'

Barnes reached into his jacket for his reading glasses, then perched them on the bridge of his nose to better see the picture. 'I thought he looked worried, myself. He kept quiet while we were speaking to Sutton but his eyes were busy.'

Kay waved them back to their seats. 'All right. Gav – have a word with some of our colleagues in East Division. See if anyone can shed some light about this chap and Mark Sutton. He looks established, so he's obviously been keeping his nose clean until now.'

'Will do.'

A desk phone interrupted Kay's thought processes and Carys leapt from her seat to hurry across the room and answer it.

The detective constable's voice fell to a murmur when she plucked the phone from the cradle, and Kay turned to Philip Parker.

'How are the statements going from the office workers at the software company?'

'They're all in HOLMES, guv,' said the young police constable. 'I've cross-referenced them with the statements we got from the other businesses opposite, but no-one saw anything suspicious at any time. We also got hold of CCTV footage from the council for the period between April and October when the software company took over the lease.'

'Nothing?'

'Sorry, no.'

'Guv!'

Kay caught sight of Carys hurtling between the desks towards her. 'What's up?'

Before the detective constable had time to answer, and to Kay's astonishment, Adam appeared at the doorway to the incident room, his face ashen.

Carys beckoned to her. 'Guv, I need a word please. It's urgent.'

'Barnes, can you take over?'

Kay didn't wait for a response and instead pushed past one of the uniformed sergeants on the team and hurried to where Carys hovered behind a row of chairs.

'What's going on?'

In reply, Carys thrust Kay's handbag at her, and then shoved her coat into her arms. 'You need to go, guv. Now.'

Kay let herself be ushered from the room by the younger detective, her thoughts only catching up with the woman's words as she reached Adam.

'What are you doing here?'

'Abby's been trying to phone you for the last thirty minutes. We need to go. It's your father,' he said. 'He's had a heart attack.'

.

FOURTEEN

Kay sniffed, then turned her head to watch the side of an articulated truck as Adam accelerated past it, so that he wouldn't see her cry.

He had enough to worry about; the traffic on the M25 was atrocious, the wind whipping debris across the eight lanes and into the verges on either side.

Rain beat against the windscreen, a persistent stream of water that fought against the wipers and caused rivulets to escape across the passenger window.

Her body leaned into the seat belt she wore as Adam applied the brakes, a soft curse under his breath.

After turning up at the incident room, he'd taken her by the arm and steered her towards his vehicle that was parked outside on double yellow lines, then stuck his finger in the air at a driver who honked his horn as they ripped open the doors, before pulling away from the kerb at such speed that Kay's head had slammed into the seat rest before she'd had a chance to fasten her seat belt.

'I can't believe she didn't call my desk phone,' said Kay.

'She was probably panicking.'

Kay choked back her anger. She wasn't going to take out her frustration on Adam.

She turned around to see his jaw set, his eyes focused ahead on the traffic that streamed before them.

'The bloody Leatherhead junction never changes,' he said under his breath. 'Come on. Move, people.'

'I can take over when you get tired. We've got a long way to go yet.'

'I'm not letting you anywhere near this steering wheel the state you're in.'

Kay exhaled, and closed her eyes.

She knew better than to argue, and he was right after all.

Her mind was a jumble of tasks she hadn't had time to delegate to her investigation team and coaching tips she should have given to Barnes to help him in her absence. Like a torrent of water underneath it all was the thought that she'd never thanked her father for what he had done for her; that she might not get the chance.

She opened her eyes and sat forward. 'Who's looking after Cornflake?'

'Scott's taken him home with him. I was at the surgery when Abby called me, so I gave him my house key and used the spare one to get indoors and grab our stuff. Stop worrying about the gerbil, Kay. He's going to be fine.'

Kay mumbled a response and then checked her mobile again.

As she'd hurried from the incident room, she'd realised her sister had phoned three times, each call going through to voicemail as Kay led her team through the late afternoon briefing. She'd tried to phone Abby as they had left Maidstone once she'd gulped back the sobs that had wracked her the moment they'd reached the M20, but her sister hadn't responded.

Instead, she'd had to listen to a cheery voicemail to leave a message after the tone, the noise from Kay's two nieces screeching with laughter in the background tearing at her heart.

Was it a bad signal, or was her sister ignoring her?

Since then, the screen remained blank. No new messages, no missed calls.

'They're probably in a part of the hospital that doesn't have a mobile signal.'

Adam's voice cut through her thoughts, and she dropped the phone into her bag.

'Maybe.'

The satellite navigation system in the car beeped once, and Kay's eyes fell to the display on the dashboard. 'It says to avoid the M4. There's a multi-vehicle accident.'

'Where?'

'East of Newbury.'

'All right.' Adam indicated and swerved out into the overtaking lane, the vehicle picking up speed. 'We'll go via Reading and cut cross-country. By the time we sit in traffic and work our way over to Swindon it won't make much difference anyway.'

Kay watched the traffic in the slower lanes pass by in a blur of taillights, the rain only ceasing to thunder against the roof of the 4x4 when they went under bridges, blue sign posts pointing out destinations she hadn't visited in years.

She closed her eyes.

When had she last seen her father?

She had spoken to him on the phone only weeks

ago; they had drifted into the habit of him calling her on a Tuesday afternoon when her mother went out with a friend of hers as a way to talk freely without her mother's knowledge.

Her mother hadn't invited them to Christmas dinner.

A year ago, she had told her parents about the miscarriage she had suffered while being subjected to a Professional Standards investigation that had been unjustified. The problem was, she had kept it from them for a year before that, and the already tumultuous relationship she'd had with her mother had deteriorated to the point where they no longer spoke to each other.

Kay clenched her fist, digging her nails into her palm to fight against the sickness that threatened to engulf her.

Her mother knew how much Kay's father meant to her, and it was obvious that she had deliberately chosen to keep her eldest daughter in the dark about his health.

Only a few months ago, her father had been rushed into hospital with chest pains. He had been lucky that time – the doctor treating him had put it down to an elevated case of heartburn, but if Abby hadn't phoned her to tell her, she'd have never known. Her mother kept to her vow of silence when it came to freezing out Kay from her life, and her father never talked about his health.

She groaned, realising she was becoming paranoid.

Adam reached out for her hand and clutched her fingers for a moment before his hand wrapped around the steering wheel once more.

'Hang in there.'

Kay closed her eyes and nodded, a fat tear rolling over her cheek.

FIFTEEN

Kay hurried towards the automatic doors of the emergency wing, and paused with ill-concealed impatience as the glass swished open.

The atmosphere struck her as one of fear tinged with an irrepressible undertone of efficiency as staff worked to calm traumatised patients and family members alike.

'Over here.'

Adam wrapped his fingers around her arm and steered her across the tiled floor to a reception desk, the administrative personnel doing their best to direct people towards the right wards and deal with an onslaught of paperwork at the same time.

The moment a woman put her phone down, Adam turned on the charm and smiled.

'I can see you're busy, so I'll keep this brief. We have a family member, Phillip Hunter, who was rushed here earlier today with a suspected heart attack. We were wondering where we might find him?'

The woman provided directions, and Adam spun away from the counter, pulling Kay along with him.

He set a fast pace through the maze of corridors that weaved through the large hospital complex, but Kay's height gave her the advantage of being able to keep up with him as they negotiated gurneys with patients and hospital staff dashing from one ward to the next.

As they rounded a corner, a cry of surprise reached her ears before her sister, Abby barrelled into her.

'You're here.'

Kay pulled her into a fierce hug, then raised her gaze to see the rest of her small family standing outside a set of double doors.

Her mother's mouth twisted into a moue of disappointment. 'So. You made it here, then. Are you sure they can spare you, back at the police station?'

'They're fine.' Kay pushed down her anger at the barbed comment. 'Why didn't you phone me to tell me he was so ill?'

'I never know if I have the right number for you. You're always working. I doubt that you'd have dropped everything to be with us anyway.'

'That's enough, Marion,' said Adam, his voice dangerously low. 'We've driven six hours to be here.'

He turned his attention to Abby and gave her a quick peck on the cheek before turning to her husband, Silas, and shaking his hand. 'Any news?'

'The doctors are with him. We're waiting for an update,' said Abby, reaching for Kay's hand.

Kay felt the familiar squeeze of her fingers, something Abby had done since they were kids whenever she needed reassurance. They didn't speak for a moment, and then Abby drew back and wiped at her cheeks.

'Where are the girls?' Despite the urgency of the situation, Kay couldn't help wonder where her two nieces were, and whether they were aware of their grandfather's plight.

'Liz is looking after them,' said Silas.

Kay exhaled. Her father's sister would be a perfect companion for the girls while they waited for news. 'What's going on? Why did he get rushed here?'

'They say he needs a pacemaker. That he was

lucky.' Abby sniffed. She flapped her hands in front of her face. 'Oh my God, he scared us, Kay.'

'What happened?' Kay turned to their mother, who shrugged.

'Well, if you'd been here you would've known.'

'Mum—' Abby began.

'Marion, please,' said Adam. 'Now isn't the—'

Kay's mother spun to face him and jabbed at his chest with a manicured nail. 'Stay out of this. You're not even family, so I don't know why you're here. Unless you two have finally got married without telling me?'

A shocked silence followed her outburst, broken only when Silas cleared his throat and placed his hand on his mother-in-law's arm.

'Stop it,' he said. 'That's out of order.'

'You know what? Enough of this. Mum – if you can't be civil, then I suggest me and Abby speak alone.' Kay turned to Adam. 'Care to join us for a coffee? I think I saw a vending machine down the corridor.'

'Sounds good to me.'

Kay turned her back on her mother and Silas, then looped her arm through Adam's and set off, not waiting to see if her sister was joining them.

She relaxed slightly at the echo of Abby's

expensive heels on the tiled floor behind her as she pushed through the double doors away from the emergency ward, then slowed as she reached the corner next to the nurse's station.

'If you're going to storm out, then at least do it slowly,' Abby grumbled. 'These heels are killing me.'

Kay loosened her grip on Adam and leaned against the wall, crossing her arms over her chest.

'What the hell is the matter with her?' she exploded. 'You'd think that after everything Dad's been through, she'd be able to rein it in.'

'It's probably the stress.' Adam jostled his jeans pocket before extracting a handful of change and proceeded to feed it into the vending machine.

Abby snorted. 'It's probably the fact she's a bitch.'

'It must've been bad lately, for you to say that,' said Kay.

'Honestly, I don't know what's gotten into her. She should be grateful you two travelled half the night to be here.'

'Maybe she's scared,' said Adam, handing them both a plastic cup filled to the brim with a dark viscous liquid. 'Fear can bring out the worst in people, and she's probably not coping that well.'

Kay took one of the drinks from him. 'Thanks.

And you're being too gracious – especially after what she said to you.'

He winked. 'I can handle her. What happened to your dad, Abby? Has this been going on for a while?'

'He's been having regular checks with his local doctor,' said Abby, her voice dull with shock. 'He's always told us that it was nothing though. Then, he collapsed today while he and Mum were out shopping. Someone from the supermarket phoned for the ambulance. I spoke with the paramedic who was on the crew that brought him in – they've been back here twice more tonight with different patients. If the manager of the place hadn't had the foresight to use the defibrillator they have there, he wouldn't... he might have—'

Kay passed her coffee to Adam and wrapped her arms around her younger sister's shoulders.

'He's here though, so he's in safe hands, Abby. You mentioned a pacemaker?'

Abby nodded as she drew away, then fished into her jacket for a paper tissue. 'Yes. They say he's stable now and talking with the care team who are looking after him. Apparently they're going to monitor him overnight and see if they can operate in the morning.'

'Can we see him?'

'Mum's been in, about an hour ago. The doctor told me and Silas it's probably better to let him rest tonight and then we can see him in the morning after the operation. Do you want to do the same?'

Kay turned to Adam, who nodded.

'Absolutely. I've got to make arrangements at the clinic for the rest of the weekend, but we can find a motel nearby and come back in the morning.'

'And I'll have to phone the station,' said Kay. She reached out for Abby's hand once more.

'But, we're family. And we're staying.'

SIXTEEN

Kay stood on the threshold of the motel room, her mind working overtime.

Somehow, in between fielding the phone call from Abby and picking up Kay from the police station, Adam had had the foresight to pack an overnight case.

'I don't know if I've picked the right things for you,' he said as he swiped the key card across the door handle and pushed it open. 'I wasn't thinking straight.'

She ran her palm over his back as he led the way into the room. 'It doesn't matter. Whatever's in here will be fine. Thank you.'

Adam stepped across to the window and pulled

the curtains to shut out a night sky lashed with heavy rainfall, then ran a hand through his wet hair.

'I'm going to give Scott a call, let him know he's in charge for the time being. At least until we know how your dad's doing.'

'Will he be okay on his own?'

Adam shrugged. 'He'll have to be. There's nothing we can do about it, is there?' He smiled to soften his words. 'You should do the same. Write off the weekend with your lot so you can concentrate on what's going on here.'

Kay shrugged off her jacket and hung it over the back of one of the chairs in the small suite, ignoring the water that dripped onto the thin carpet.

Pulling her mobile phone out of her bag, she frowned at the display.

'Don't worry, I brought a charger,' said Adam. He kicked off his shoes and plumped up the pillows on one side of the bed, then swung his legs up and hit the speed dial on the phone. He winked as his colleague answered.

Kay sank into a chair and scrolled through her phone until she found the number she sought, wondering how she would cope if she were on her own right now.

Adam's calm demeanour washed over her enough that, for a moment at least, she could concentrate.

Barnes picked up on the first ring. 'Kay?'

'Hi.'

'What's happening?'

'Dad's had a heart attack, but he's in recovery. They're talking about a pacemaker.' She heard the tremble in her voice as she spoke. 'We're having to stay in Swindon over the weekend until we know how he's doing, so—'

'Not a problem,' said Barnes. 'The whole team is scheduled to work over the weekend as you requested, so we can keep the investigation moving forward.'

Kay released the breath she'd been holding. 'You're a star, Ian.'

'You'd do the same for me. Do you want a quick update?'

'Yes, that'd be good, thanks.'

She smiled. Her detective sergeant might have sounded brusque and efficient to anybody else, but she knew him too well and could spot the emotion in his voice.

He knew that the only way to stop her falling apart was to keep her mind busy, and as he updated her about the end of the briefing she'd left so abruptly, her thoughts turned to the management of the investigation.

She knew the next twenty-four hours would test all her abilities as a leader.

She had to trust her team; she had to learn to delegate.

Evaluating each task, making suggestions to Barnes's planned course of action, and encouraging him where she felt he needed coaching, she helped him plot a way forward that would keep up the momentum in her absence.

When that was done she ended the call, plugged in her phone charger next to the bedside table, and signalled to Adam that she was going to shower.

His voice carried through into the bathroom as he discussed with Scott which appointments to cancel and what animals required careful monitoring. Laughter ensued as Adam listened to his employee, and Kay smiled as she undressed and then stepped under the hot jets of water.

However, as she let the stress from the past few hours wash away from her skin, a melancholy seized her.

Outside of her home life and work, she realised she had nothing.

No friends to call when life threw a wrench in the

works. No-one outside of the police who she could talk to about—

She stopped, her hands soapy with shampoo as she froze.

Talk to about what?

She lived for her work. It was why she had thrown herself into proving her innocence when challenged by a Professional Standards allegation. It was why she gave up her weekends to lead major investigations and set an example to junior colleagues.

Adam's work often meant he worked unsociable hours, too, and she realised as she began to scrub at her hair with renewed vigour that they both lived for their work. They enjoyed what they did, but what little choice had they left themselves with?

A familiar sense of dread began to claw at her chest and she reached out for the faucet, twisting it shut and wrapping a large towel under her arms before tucking it in.

She wiped at the condensation that clung to the mirror, then peered at the frightened face that stared back at her.

What if something happened to Adam?

What would she do?

Who could she turn to for support?

She sniffed, then tried to clear the thought. Drying

herself, she pulled on fresh clothes and stepped out into the bedroom.

Adam ended his call and met her gaze, a circumspect expression on his face.

'This is crazy, Hunter. We can't go on like this. We've got to learn to let go, haven't we?'

She bit her lip, and then reached out for his hand, lost for words.

SEVENTEEN

Kay felt Adam's hand slip around her fingers as she pushed open the door to the ward thirty-six hours later and crossed the tiled floor towards a bed near the window, a curtain separating its occupant from the others in the room.

Her breath caught in her throat as she peered around it at the foot of the bed.

Her father was sitting upright, but his face was the palest she'd ever seen.

His mane of white hair stuck out in different directions, and his eyes bore testimony to the fight his body had been through in the past three days.

Still, he managed a faint smile at the sight of his eldest daughter.

'It must be urgent if you've both managed to skive off from work.'

'Oh, Dad.' Kay rushed towards him and gave him a gentle hug. 'You scared the hell out of us.'

He held her tight, and then eased her away, shaking hands with Adam.

'How are you, Phil?'

'Sore. Like I've been kicked by a horse.'

'We would've been in yesterday but they delayed your operation and kept us away.'

Kay's father shrugged. 'Staff shortage, apparently. One of those things.' He reached up and tapped the left side of his chest. 'Got a new friend now.'

He pulled down the collar of his gown and Kay winced at the bandages that covered his chest, purple and yellow bruising covering his shoulder.

'You're going to be all right now, yes?' she managed.

'As well as I can be. The surgeon came around about half an hour ago and said the operation went well. They'll be keeping me in here a few days to make sure I don't get up to mischief.' He reached out for her hand. 'I'm glad you both came.'

'Dad, we wouldn't be anywhere else. You know that.'

'I know, but I'm fine now. Abby said you're in the middle of a murder investigation?'

Kay nodded. 'I am, but I've got a good team working with me. They'll have it under control.'

Her father smiled. 'But there's another family who needs you now, isn't there? A family who need some answers. And that's what you do best, Kay.'

She sighed. 'I wish Mum would see it like that.'

'Your mother will never understand, kiddo. It's not in her nature.' He raised his gaze to where Adam hovered at the end of the bed. 'I imagine things are busy at the clinic as well, aren't they?'

'Under control, Phil. Scott's coping without me.'

'Coping, yes but these people depend on the two of you.' Kay's father shifted his weight, then held up his hand as Kay moved to his side. 'I'm fine. It looks worse than it is.'

'Are you telling us to get lost, Dad?' She kept her tone light, but couldn't hide her frown.

He laughed. 'Not in a bad way, no. But look around you – I'm getting the best care possible, I'm out of danger and in two or three days they're going to kick me out of here. What are you going to do if you hang around? Mope about worrying what's going on back home?'

'Well—'

'Exactly.' He cocked his head at approaching footsteps, a voice reaching Kay's ears as his eyes locked with hers. 'And that's your mother. I take it from your sister that things got a bit heated when you got here the other night?'

Kay bit her lip. 'You could say that.'

Her father patted her hand, then made a shooing gesture. 'Go on. It's good to see you both, and thank you for coming. But I don't think the ward sister will appreciate the fireworks display if you and your mother spend too much time in each other's company.'

'If you're sure, Dad?'

He smiled. 'I'm sure. I'll give you a call next week.'

KAY'S MOOD was one of retrospect as she and Adam drove back towards Kent after a hurried lunch with Abby and Silas.

Her father's words went around in her head; he had always been the more supportive of her parents, but she wondered if he knew how close to the truth his observations had been.

She and Adam hadn't stopped checking their

phones all day yesterday, and she'd been almost tempted to use the business centre at the motel to log in to a computer to check her emails.

Almost.

A wry smile crossed her lips as she recalled their conversation.

'What are you thinking?' said Adam, before pulling away from a set of traffic lights and crossing the busy junction.

'Just what Dad said to us. He's right. We don't do anything else *except* work. We're not very good at delegating, either are we?'

'I reckon, once you've got this investigation out of the way, we should have a break,' said Adam. 'A proper one. I mean weeks, not days.'

Kay kicked off her shoes and wiggled her toes. 'I can almost feel the sand.'

'Where do you fancy going?'

'Anywhere. Preferably somewhere without a phone signal or Wi-Fi.'

Adam laughed. 'You wouldn't last three days without a phone signal.'

'I'm willing to try.'

'All right. How about a remote corner of Thailand?'

'Sounds good. We've never been to Asia.'

She frowned as her phone began to vibrate inside her bag, and leaned forward to fish it out.

'Like I said, you wouldn't last,' said Adam.

'Very funny.' She hit the "answer" button. 'DI Hunter.'

'Guv, it's Barnes. I'm about to head off for the day, so I thought you might appreciate an update. I've got Gavin here with me on speakerphone. How's your dad?'

'He's recovering, Ian – thanks.' Kay shifted in her seat and watched the countryside flash by. 'He's had a pacemaker fitted and the doctors are pleased with how the operation went. Lots of rest and recovery for him, though. He's not out of danger yet. How are things there?'

She listened as Barnes ran through the briefings he'd given to the team in her absence and the meagre information that had come to light, his frustration palpable at the lack of progress.

'There is one more thing,' said Barnes, his voice hesitant.

'What's that?'

'Simon Winter phoned from the mortuary at Derwent Valley. He said Lucas has managed to catch up over the past few days and that he'll do the post mortem on our victim first thing tomorrow. I can go, if you want. You probably won't know what's going on there with your dad for a day or so, will you?'

Kay glanced across at Adam as he rubbed at his eyes, trying to suppress a yawn as he merged with the fast-moving traffic.

'Tell you what,' she said. 'We're on our way back to Kent now, so I'll attend the post mortem. Could you do tomorrow's briefing for me, though?'

Adam glanced across at her and rolled his eyes.

She tried to shrug off the guilt at the prospect of returning to the investigation so soon after her father's health scare, focusing on the tasks at hand instead. Despite what she'd said to Adam only moments before about delegating, as Senior Investigating Officer it was her preference to attend a post mortem simply so that she could listen to what the Home Office pathologist discovered rather than read it from a report. She had learned from Sharp that it was often the best way, even though the whole procedure could be unpleasant.

'No problem about the briefing,' said Barnes. 'I can give you an update when you're back here.'

'Great, thanks. Gavin—' Kay raised her voice so the detective constable could hear her better over the roar of the car engine. 'It's your turn, Piper. I'll meet you at the station at seven o'clock and then we'll drive over to the mortuary together.'

The detective constable sighed. 'I guess I won't be having breakfast tomorrow, then.'

EIGHTEEN

Gavin set his jaw upon meeting Kay at the police station the next morning and followed her out to the car without complaint, but his complexion remained ashen as they travelled along the M20 towards the hospital.

He had always struggled with the fact that attending a post mortem was vital to understanding a victim's fatal injuries in order to work an investigation, and Kay had undertaken to guide him through the process wherever possible.

She simply couldn't do anything to calm his nerves or the sickness that wracked him every time he had to attend, though, and leaving Barnes to shepherd the younger detective through the doors of the laboratory where Lucas Anderson worked would only leave Gavin more traumatised, she was sure.

'How are you holding up?' she said, glancing sideways at him as they walked across the asphalt towards the doors of the building.

'It doesn't get any easier.'

'Thought you were a bit quiet on the way over.'

'How's your dad, if you don't mind me asking, guv?'

'Gave us one hell of a fright, to be honest,' said Kay, 'but his doctor says he's strong and should make a good recovery in time.'

'That's great news, guv.'

Gavin held open the door and followed her over to the reception desk.

Kay frowned at the sound of wind chimes as Gavin scrawled his signature underneath hers.

'Relaxation music?' she said. 'Since when has Lucas started playing that in here?'

The twenty-something receptionist rolled her eyes and took the sign-in sheet back from Gavin. 'Last week. I told him there was no point – I mean, it's not like it's going to do his patients any good, is it?'

'Now, now.'

The Home Office pathologist stood at the door to the mortuary, his mask pulled down to his neck and his mouth twitching. 'It provides a relaxing introduction to anyone visiting us.'

'That's what you think,' said Gavin, his voice gruff. 'My dentist has this same playlist. I'm never going there again.'

Kay laughed and steered the younger detective away from the desk. 'Let's go. The sooner we hear what Lucas has to tell us, the sooner I can get you back to the station.'

She gestured to the pathologist that they'd be with him shortly, then found the ladies' changing room.

Placing her valuables in a locker and pocketing the key, she took a fresh set of protective coveralls from a plastic bag and pulled them over her blouse and trousers.

She hummed under her breath as she dressed; nothing recognisable, simply something to take her mind off what might be waiting for her on the gurney behind the doors to the mortuary.

Tugging her ankle boots back on, she opened the door to find Gavin pacing the corridor.

He stopped when she appeared, squaring his shoulders. 'Ready, guv?'

'Lead the way.'

The door through to the mortuary opened as they

approached and Simon Winter, Lucas's assistant appeared.

'Good timing,' he said, his pale eyes stark under a dark fringe. 'We've almost finished.'

He stood to one side to let them through, and Kay began to breathe in shallow breaths to alleviate the smell that threatened to overwhelm her senses.

'Over here, come on,' said Lucas, and waved them across to the examination table.

Bright lights flickered to life above it, illuminating the shrunken corpse laid out, its ragged clothing already prised away and bagged for further examination by Harriet's team.

As she drew closer, Kay was reminded of an exhibit at the British Museum she'd seen several years ago and recalled the indignity that had swept over her as crowds jostled to gawp at the shrivelled body.

It had seemed so disrespectful.

Her gaze followed Simon's progress as he began to gather up the bags, and then she turned to the Home Office pathologist. 'I don't suppose there were any personal effects tucked into seams, anything to tell us who he was?'

'I'm afraid not. No signs of rings on his fingers,

nothing in his pockets, and no previous injuries to trace back through medical records.'

'A real mystery man,' said Gavin, shoving a tube of menthol vapour rub back in his jacket pocket and rubbing his finger above his top lip.

'Unfortunately for you, yes,' said Lucas.

'What *can* you tell us?' said Kay, fighting down a sense of desperation that clawed at her guts. 'Surely you've got something we can work with?'

'Steady on. I'll take you through what I do know following my examination and then we'll work out what's missing.'

Kay nodded, and forced herself to relax. Lucas had a point – there was no sense in worrying about evidence she didn't have until she'd learned what he had gleaned from the post mortem.

He beckoned her closer to the table until she and Gavin were poised next to the victim's head.

'I was right about the trauma wound to his head,' he said, cradling the man's skull while he ran his little finger down the indentation. 'This isn't what killed him.'

Lucas moved to the left, then reached out and lifted the victim's arm, turning the hand until the fingertips were exposed.

'Did you manage to get prints?' said Kay.

'Not from this hand. Remember I said at the scene that the tips were smooth?'

'Someone at the station suggested he might've been a guitar player,' said Gavin.

'It's not a terrible theory.'

'But it's not right?' said Kay.

'No – I don't think so.' Lucas lowered the victim's arm and gestured to the man's feet. 'Come over here.'

Kay tried to ignore the shrunken skin that covered the man's form, and concentrated on the long bones of the man's toes as she drew near.

'What am I looking for?'

Lucas waited until she and Gavin were next to him, and then pointed to a misshapen black mark on the sole of the left foot.

Gavin's brow furrowed. 'Is that a tattoo?'

Lucas managed a smile. 'That would be a first for me. No – it's an exit wound. A scorch mark.'

Kay took a step back. 'No fingerprints, and an exit wound on his foot. He was electrocuted, wasn't he?'

'Well done, Hunter. Yes, you're right.'

'Is that what killed him?'

Lucas reached across and pulled a brightly coloured sheet over the mummified remains, leaving the head exposed. 'Yes. I'm ninety per cent certain of that.'

'And he sustained the crack to the back of his head afterwards?' said Gavin. He gestured to the shrivelled form, the empty eye sockets pale under the laboratory lights. 'I mean, when he was already dead?'

'I believe so, yes,' said Lucas. He tugged the sheet across the victim's face and began to remove his gloves.

Kay exhaled. 'So, did you get any fingerprints off his right hand?'

'I've emailed the results to you and your records officer.'

'Fantastic, thanks.'

'That building was crawling with contractors and site security during the redevelopment works, so why didn't anyone report it?' said Gavin.

'The carpet fitters mentioned to Hughes in their original statements that they were delayed one morning because the power was out in the building,' said Kay. 'Maybe our victim here was electrocuted and someone else hid his body to cover up the fact they'd been there.'

'But John Brancourt says he employed Sutton Site Security to keep a watch on the place after they threatened him.'

Kay's gaze returned to the form under the sheet

and a shiver crossed her shoulders. 'Well, he didn't end up in that cavity of his own volition, Gav. Someone was there when he died and knew what happened to him. All we have to do is find out who that was.'

NINETEEN

Upon returning to the police station on Palace Avenue, Kay elected to interview Tom Walsh, the carpet fitters' supervisor.

Carys managed to track down both carpet fitters before they'd reached the pub after an early finish from a job they'd been working on in Leeds village, and now they waited in separate interview rooms while Kay and Gavin faced their boss across the table in interview room three.

'Thanks for coming in,' said Kay. 'To begin with, could you tell us about your job?'

The forty-nine-year-old tugged at his collar, adjusted a half-smoked cigarette behind his ear, and then folded his arms on the table.

'I've been working for the flooring company for

about fifteen years,' he began. 'Worked my way up and then started training the apprentices. About eight years ago, they got me supervising some of the bigger jobs. Ones for corporate clients like Hill that made up for lulls in the domestic work.'

'Do you enjoy it?'

He shrugged. 'S'all right, I suppose.'

'How did you become involved with the work at the Petersham Building over the summer?'

'We'd done work for John Brancourt before,' he said, 'so we didn't have to tender for the job. He got permission from the owner, Hill, to employ us based on past results. So, once our sales team had a note of Hill's preferences for the carpets and underlay he placed the order and then Brancourt told him when we'd need to be there. You know – in line with the project schedule.'

'How much time did you spend at the site?'

'A couple of days to start off with, to make sure the lads were all right. Sometimes you get to a place and the measurements haven't been taken right or the client's changed his mind during the other works so you turn up and all the angles are wrong. Luckily with this job, it was a simple case of checking the original measurements and then letting the lads get on with it.

After that, I went back once a week until the job was done.'

'What is John Brancourt like to deal with?'

'He's a good bloke. Old school, know what I mean? He does a good job trusting us to do our work and fielding calls from Hill.'

'Oh? Does Alexander Hill tend to cause problems?'

'No, I didn't say that. He's just one of those blokes who always has to know what's going on. Likes to keep an eye on things on site. Doesn't like it when the schedule gets behind. It's his investment, after all.'

'Was he ever aggressive in any way towards you or your men?'

'God, no.' His mouth quirked. 'There were enough clauses in the contract that could hurt us if things went wrong. He'd never have to lift a finger.'

Kay ended the interview, then led the way to the next room and gestured to Gavin to begin the next round of questions with Michael Blake.

Blake had been slouched in his seat when they'd entered, but now sat fully alert, his face eager.

'Anything I can do to help,' he said as Gavin finished reading the formal interview caution. 'Anything at all.'

'Who assigned the work to you on a daily basis?' said Gavin.

'Our supervisor, Tom,' said Michael. 'We'd have a quick chat on site with him when we got there each morning, make sure there were no problems from the previous day or find out if there were any changes to the rooms we were scheduled to work in.'

Kay opened the manila folder in front of her and slid a page across the table to the carpet fitter.

'This is the daily worksheet you provided on the day that the underlay in the office above the breakout area had been fitted, but that the carpets couldn't be laid because the power was out. What happened?'

Michael glanced at the worksheet before shoving it back towards her. 'It happens sometimes – minor delays. Nothing to worry about as far as the contract was concerned 'cause we simply went and worked in another room at the building that day. The power was back on within twenty-four hours. It was only a dodgy old trip switch that had blown in the main fuse box but it took a while to find an electrician to get back to the site at short notice.'

'When you went back to work in the office above the kitchen area, did you see or perhaps sense anything unusual?'

Michael shuddered. 'No, and it creeps me out to think we were working right above where he was.'

'Did the underlay look disturbed in any way?'

'No – that's the thing. We'd pinned it down two days before, and I would've noticed if anything was wrong. That's the thing with old buildings, you see – you expect the floors to be uneven. With that place, they'd redesigned the interior so the original floor had been ripped out. The new one was perfect. One of the easiest jobs I've worked on around here.'

'You said in your original statement that you finished working in that room and the offices below a couple of days later,' said Kay, reading the photocopied text in her hand. 'Did you notice any unusual smells while you were working?'

Michael shook his head. 'I've been thinking about that since the copper asked me earlier this week. There was nothing. I mean, something like that – well, you'd think it'd stink, right?'

Another shudder wracked the man's shoulders and Kay felt a surge of sympathy for him.

No doubt since the news broke, he and his work colleague had been wondering "what if" on a regular basis. His horror certainly appeared genuine.

Satisfied that she would learn no more from Michael Blake, Kay terminated the interview, thanked him for his time and let Gavin show him back through to the reception area.

When the detective constable returned, he sat opposite her with a loud sigh.

'So, what do you think, guv?'

Kay closed the folder and rested her hands on it. 'We'll talk to the other carpet fitter, Andy James, next to close that loop but I don't think we're going to learn anything new,' she said. 'Whoever hid our victim's body in the cavity knew what they were doing and, even if they didn't, from how Michael describes the state of the new flooring it wouldn't have taken an expert to pin the underlay back in place afterwards. I'll check with Harriet and her team, but my guess is the composition of the underlay masked any initial smell of decay and then, like Lucas said, nature took its course and the body became mummified relatively quickly.'

'You don't suspect Michael or his colleague, then?'

'No.' Kay tapped her finger on the folder. 'Everything he's told us matches the worksheets on file. Unless Andy James tells us differently, I don't think this lot had anything to do with our victim. And we need to monitor Alexander Hill. Have a look through the paperwork and see if we've got a copy of the contract for the carpet fitters. Find out how much Hill could hurt them by if they didn't finish on time.' Kay pushed back her chair and rose to her feet, tucking the folder under her arm. 'All right – where is Andy?'

'Next door.'

'Grab a coffee for him, Gav – he's been waiting a while.'

'Guv.'

TWENTY

By the time they'd returned to the incident room, Gavin's features had lost the peaky colour he'd been wearing all day and the young detective constable was shovelling a double-sized hamburger into his mouth as Kay held open the door for him.

'Bloody hell, it's like a gannet,' said Barnes, thrusting a wad of paperwork at Kay as she passed his chair.

'Tell me about it. That's the second one he's had,' she said. 'The canteen will run out at this rate.'

'I didn't have any breakfast, guv – remember?' said Gavin between mouthfuls. He swallowed. 'I don't know how you lot do it.'

Barnes winked at Kay. 'I reckon he should go every time to toughen up.'

Gavin froze, the burger halfway to his mouth. 'You're joking.'

'He is. We take turns.' Kay wagged her finger at Barnes. 'And you're next.'

Barnes emitted a theatrical groan, then gestured to the report in her hand as she sat. 'Carys has a couple of people working through the fingerprints Lucas sent through with his report. I understand that it might've been an accidental death?'

'Maybe. It sure as hell wasn't an accidental cover-up, though,' said Kay.

Carys joined them, then passed around a packet of biscuits and rolled her eyes as Gavin helped himself to three.

'We've started the database search for our victim's fingerprints,' she said. 'We're concentrating on West Kent to begin with, and then we'll take a look further afield if we don't find anything.'

'Widen the search to Sussex, Surrey and Greater London if that comes up blank,' said Kay. 'If that doesn't yield any results we might have to consider putting in a request to Interpol.'

'I hadn't even thought of the fact he might not be British,' said Gavin.

'I've drafted the paperwork,' said Carys. 'All it needs is your signature, guv, if we want to go ahead with that. A warning though – I've heard there's at least a four-week delay on getting results.'

'All right, thanks,' said Kay. 'I guess we cross our fingers that he was a local. How did uniform get on this morning interviewing the previous tenants of the building? Anything of interest?'

Carys wrinkled her nose. 'Not really. A couple of the employees from the bloodstock racing agency were a bit pissed off about losing their jobs because the owner relocated out of the area, and because the employees were on temporary contracts they weren't compensated. I don't think they had anything to do with hiding that body though. The woman who owns the boutique is now working from home running a home shopping business and told Hughes and Parker that she's never been happier because she doesn't have to deal with the public face to face.'

'Sounds like the construction work didn't ruffle any feathers, then.'

'Oh, I wouldn't say that,' said Carys. 'There were a few small protests that happened at the time of the various redevelopments works around town – nothing came through here because uniform dealt with it and there were only a couple of minor infringements that happened. It's just that I can't find anything in the statements to suggest that anyone uniform spoke to had motive to kill or hide our victim.'

'What about DNA?' said Kay. 'Has anyone started to coordinate with Missing Persons to see if we have a match there?'

'We started that at the same time as cross-referencing the fingerprints,' said Barnes. 'Of course, if our victim was adopted—'

'Then it's a wasted task,' finished Kay. 'Yes, I know but we have to rule it all out.'

'Surely somebody is looking for him,' said Gavin. 'I mean, he's been in that ceiling for, what – five or six months at least?'

'Six and a half,' said Carys. She wandered over to her desk and returned with a copy of an invoice. 'This is a copy of the final bill from the carpet fitters dated mid-July that Tom Walsh gave to me. They'd finished the week before.'

'And no-one's reported any sign of disturbance in that carpet, so he was definitely placed in the floor before that went down,' said Kay.

She picked up a photograph of the mummified body from the papers Carys gave to her. 'You poor bastard. Electrocuted, and then shoved into a building cavity.'

She sighed and handed back the photograph and

documentation to Carys, then ran her hand through her hair and glared across the room at the whiteboard depicting the timeline of events that were known to date.

'All right. Get onto John Brancourt and set up an interview with him this afternoon if you can. Tomorrow morning at the latest – I don't care where he is or what he's doing, I want to speak with him.'

'Guv, you might want to see this first.' Phillip Parker hurried between the desks towards her and handed her a page still warm from the printer.

She took it from him without a word, her brow creasing as she scanned the lines of text across the page. She emitted a gasp when she read the last words.

'Shit.'

'What is it?' said Carys.

'Fingerprint results.' Kay flipped the page around and held it up so Barnes and Carys could read it, then raised her gaze to where Parker stood, his face eager. 'Are you absolutely sure about this? There's no mistake?'

'No mistake, guv. I got Sergeant Hughes to check it.'

'What's going on?' Gavin pushed back his chair. 'What's that?'

'The fingerprints match those of Damien Brancourt,' said Kay, handing him the report. She brushed past him and swept her jacket off the back of her chair. 'Barnes, with me. We'd better go and break the news to John Brancourt and his wife.'

TWENTY-ONE

'What the hell was Damien Brancourt doing at a protest twelve months ago?'

Barnes turned over the photocopied page of the original charge sheet as Kay indicated right and turned into a narrow lane off the Loose Road.

'He must have been, what – twenty-three? Twenty-four?' He folded the page and shoved it in the inner pocket of his jacket. 'Old enough to know better, anyway.'

'Don't you think it's strange that he was at a protest about the redevelopment works?' said Kay. 'Especially as his father was project managing the bank building renovations?'

'Think he was doing it just to antagonise his dad?'

'Maybe. Something worth bearing in mind. I take it he wasn't convicted?'

'No.'

'Any trouble after that?'

'No. Not until he turned up dead, anyway.'

'Remind me to ask Carys go through the records and see who else was arrested with him. I'd like to hear what they've got to say for themselves.'

Barnes flipped open his notebook and scrawled across the page, before snapping it shut and pointing out of the windscreen at a converted barn that came into view as they rounded a bend. 'This is the place.'

'Very nice, too,' Kay murmured as she drove between two brick pillars and then braked outside a floor-to-roof height window arrangement.

She craned her neck as she climbed from the car and walked across the gravel towards an oak front door, but realised that darkened privacy glass had been fitted to the frames.

Checking that Barnes was ready, she reached out and pressed a button to the left of the double doors, noticing a small camera set into the wall above it.

She kept her face impassive, then turned back to Barnes. 'It's one of those security features you can link to your mobile phone. They might not be in—'

Kay fell silent as a locking mechanism was

released, and then one side of the doors swung inwards and a woman in dark blue jeans and a black shirt appeared, her expression perplexed.

'Yes? What do you want?'

Kay held up her warrant card. 'Mrs Brancourt? I'm Detective Inspector Kay Hunter. I wondered if I could speak with you and your husband?'

The woman peered at the card through reading glasses, then rested her shoulder against the doorframe. 'What's this about?'

'Is your husband in, Mrs Brancourt?' Barnes stepped forward, his voice calm. 'We'd like to speak to both of you, please.'

The woman sighed, then pulled the door open. 'Come in, then.'

Kay wiped her feet on the doormat, then followed her across slate tiles.

To her right, a timber staircase led up to a minstrel gallery that overlooked the hallway, while to her left a large fireplace glowed from a bundle of logs that blazed behind a glass window. Heat washed over her as she passed, and left her with a longing to remain in the hallway.

'Who is it, Annabelle?'

John Brancourt's voice resonated from further along the hallway, and his wife gestured to Kay and

Barnes to follow her through a doorway that led to a large bespoke kitchen.

At one end, a modern range gleamed from within a brick recess. The surrounding cabinetry had been left in its natural colours, brightening the walls while a large table filled the far end of the room, a threadbare sofa next to it lending a rustic charm to the space.

A chair scraped across the tiles as John Brancourt rose from where he'd been working on a laptop at the table. As he did so, Kay's attention was caught by a Border Collie that raised its head from its sleeping position on the sofa. It blinked and then closed its eyes once more as John Brancourt murmured a command to it.

Kay shook his hand, and then gestured to the table. 'Do you mind if we all sit down?'

She saw Annabelle exchanged a glance with her husband, but neither of them protested. Instead, Annabelle cleared her throat.

'Can I offer you tea, or a glass of water?'

'That won't be necessary, thank you.'

John Brancourt returned to his laptop, closed the lid and shuffled his paperwork to one side before sitting, and Annabelle joined him.

Kay chose a seat diagonally opposite them, with Barnes settling to her left.

He removed his notebook, popped the end of his ballpoint pen, and then Kay folded her hands and leaned towards the Brancourts.

'Mr and Mrs Brancourt, as you're aware the body of a male in his twenties was discovered in the ceiling cavity of the Petersham Building on the High Street in Maidstone. I'm sorry to have to tell you this, but after a fingerprint analysis we've reason to believe that the body found is that of your son, Damien.'

A silence descended on the kitchen, and then to Kay's surprise, John's features broke into a smile.

Confused, she opened her mouth to speak but he waved his hand to stop her.

'It can't be Damien,' he explained, 'because he's been in Nepal since the end of June.'

Kay exchanged a glance with Barnes, then turned back to the Brancourts. 'Are you sure?'

'Of course.' Annabelle's brow creased.

'Can you recall the day he left?'

'The twenty-eighth,' said John. 'He had an early morning flight that day so he went up to Heathrow the evening before. I dropped him off at the train station after we'd had dinner that night.'

'Did he seem concerned by anything in the weeks leading up to his trip?' said Barnes.

Annabelle smiled. 'Not at all. He was glad to be finished with his degree – I think he struggled with the last year and wanted to take a break before finding a job.'

'What was he studying?' said Kay.

'Business, with a major in project management,' said John.

Annabelle reached out for his hand and squeezed. 'He's going to follow in John's footsteps.'

'Have you heard from him since he left?' said Kay.

'No – but we don't expect to,' said John. 'He's doing some voluntary work to help rebuild earthquake-affected areas so the communications channels are out.'

'He didn't let you know he'd arrived?'

'He's twenty-four years old, detective. Twenty-five in July. He can look after himself.'

'How long is his trip going to last?' said Barnes.

'He's due back in time for Easter,' said Annabelle. 'The seventeenth of April, to be exact. Unless his flight gets delayed of course.'

'Going back to his last year at university,' said Kay. 'You say he struggled with his studies. Any chance that could be related to his being arrested at a protest twelve months ago? It is, after all, how his fingerprints were recorded on our database and then analysed.'

'Bloody idiot,' said John, shaking his head. 'He should've known better.'

'He got involved with a girl at university,' said Annabelle. 'A bad influence. Always moaning about something – save this, save that. It was her idea to join a protest about the work going on in the town. In fact, I think she might have had something to do with organising it. Damien got into some sort of scuffle outside a building being renovated near the river.'

'We've seen the charge sheet,' said Barnes. 'Damien threatened a site worker and was seen doing so by a police officer. If you were involved in the redevelopment works in town, why would your son directly threaten someone employed to guard a similar building while works were ongoing?'

John sighed. 'I've no idea. I never saw anything. Damien knew some people who worked on the various projects in the area so he might have seen something, I suppose.' He shrugged. 'Maybe that was what the altercation was about. Damien never spoke about it afterwards. Thank goodness your lot saw fit to let him off with a stern warning and nothing else.'

'We'll need the name of the girl,' said Kay.

'Julie Rowe,' said Annabelle. 'Lives with her mum out by East Malling.'

'Thanks.' Kay pulled out a DNA kit from her handbag and raised her gaze to John once more. 'I'd like to take a sample from you so our pathologist can test the results alongside those we have for our victim. Would that be okay?'

'Of course. I'm telling you though, it's not Damien. There must be a mistake in your system.'

Kay conducted the test after putting gloves on and then using a small swab to wipe the inside of John's mouth before sealing the sample and writing on the label.

She picked up her handbag and dropped the kit into it, then thanked the Brancourts.

'I'll be in touch with the results, whatever they may be,' she said as Annabelle led the way back to the front door. 'And please – if Damien does contact you, let us know?'

'Of course,' said John. 'But like Annabelle said, we don't expect to hear from him until mid-April when he's back in Kathmandu.'

'Thanks.'

Kay followed Barnes back to the car, the sound of the front door closing as she reached the vehicle.

She paused next to it. 'Ian, there isn't some sort of error in the system is there?'

'Hughes checked it, but look – maybe there is. At least we've got a sample of John's DNA that'll confirm it once and for all when we get the results.' Barnes took the keys from her and gestured towards the passenger seat. 'Hop in.'

'In light of the fact the Brancourts are adamant their son is in Nepal, it's still going to take until next week before Lucas can get any results to us from this DNA swab,' she said, closing the passenger door and wrapping the seatbelt over her chest. 'In the meantime, let's take a closer look at that protest.'

'You think maybe it's related to our victim's death?'

Kay sighed. 'Right now, Barnes, I have no idea, but it's worth a shot.'

TWENTY-TWO

Early the next morning, Kay entered the police station at the same time as Carys arrived, the younger detective unwrapping a scarf from her neck as she followed Kay through the front door before huffing on her fingers to warm them.

Kay had briefed the team on her return from the Brancourts' house with Barnes and then worked with Debbie to arrange the staff roster. She made sure her team received one day off each, but knew she wouldn't rest until the investigation ended. She would be at work every morning without fail, leading her team until she ensured justice for their victim.

As Carys held open the door for her, Kay appraised the rows of desks and stopped short.

Surprise was quickly followed by a sense of pride

as she realised every single member of her team had ignored the roster and were all present, answering telephones, calling to each other across the room and wearing an expression every bit as determined as her own.

'Morning, guv,' said Gavin as she reached her desk and threw her coat onto a hook behind the door to DCI Sharp's unused office.

'Morning. So, when were you lot planning on telling me the new roster was a waste of time?' she said, unable to keep the smile from her lips.

'Thought it'd be a nice surprise,' said Barnes. He dropped his mobile phone onto the desk next to his coffee cup and shoved a paper bag across to her, pointing at it and the cup of takeout coffee next to her computer. 'Croissant. Figured you wouldn't have eaten breakfast.'

'Thanks, Ian.' She tore open the bag, the pastry still warm, and ripped off a corner to eat as she moved towards the whiteboard and let the hum of activity envelop her.

There was no need to have a briefing this morning; all the tasks had been assigned the previous day through a mixture of reports extracted from HOLMES and Kay's own requirements as Senior Investigating Officer.

Instead, she let her mind wander as she took in the updated information she'd added the previous afternoon, running a critical eye over the investigation to date and mulling over her options for progress.

It was imperative she kept the team's energy focused and alert to anything that might help them deduce what Damien Brancourt's involvement was with the redevelopment of the Petersham Building – if their victim was indeed the project manager's son.

Yesterday's meeting with John and Annabelle Brancourt had left her unsettled, and questioning her own assertions about the victim's identity.

Kay finished the croissant as she wandered back to her desk. 'Ian, while we're waiting for the DNA results to come through from Lucas, let's work on the assumption that the Brancourts are correct and we're wrong. Double check their story about Damien travelling to Nepal – did anything come through from the Home Office, Harry?'

Sergeant Davis turned from the photocopier and shook his head. 'No, guv. I got onto someone there late yesterday, but she told me they're short on staff this week. It's unlikely I'll get a response before Monday now.'

'What about CCTV imagery from Heathrow?'

'We've got a request in with the UK Border

Agency,' said Gavin. 'I'm going to give them another call in an hour to chase it up. As soon as anything comes through, I'll get it across to Andy Grey at headquarters.'

'Thanks.' Kay listened as Gavin explained that he had spoken to the digital forensic expert the previous day, and the man had offered the services of two of his staff knowing the urgency with which Kay and her team needed the information. 'What about his passport records?'

'Still waiting for it,' said Barnes. 'I've requested the records to prove his date of departure. Annabelle Brancourt couldn't recall the airline or booking company Damien used to arrange his flights, so we've got no information with regard to that. If the Border Agency can get his passport details to us though, we might be able to work it out backwards from there.'

'Put a call through to the British Consulate in Nepal as well, Ian. If Damien was meant to be doing voluntary work in earthquake-affected communities then he may have registered with them in case of an emergency. We might as well process this from both ends of his journey. Goodness knows when the Border Agency will come back to us given their workload these days.'

'Good point, will do.' Barnes scrawled in his

notebook. 'I got hold of Amanda Miller before you arrived – she's one of the forensic financial investigators based over at headquarters. She'll be here tomorrow to start the investigation into how Sutton Site Security might be set up so we can find out if there's any substance to Alexander Hill and John Brancourt's accusations.'

'That's great, thanks. The sooner we can have her providing us with some guidance, the better.' Kay called over to Carys and waited until the detective constable neared. 'Can you go through the records with Debbie and find out who was arrested alongside Damien at the student protest? I'd like to interview them as soon as possible to hear what they've got to say – especially someone called Julie Rowe. According to Annabelle Brancourt, she's the reason Damien got into trouble in the first place.'

'No problem,' said Carys. 'Do you want to sit in on all the interviews?'

'No, that's fine – you and Debbie do them. I'll only interview Julie with you.'

Carys nodded and moved back towards her desk, pausing to speak with Debbie as she reached the police constable who was reloading the printers.

Kay turned away from the two women and wheeled her chair closer to her computer monitor, wiggling her mouse to wake the screen and then ran her eyes down the list of emails that had appeared that morning.

She bit back a groan – she was gradually getting used to the increased management workload that took up a lot of her daily role, and had worked out a system of prioritising what she needed to do and delegating the rest.

She took a deep gulp of her coffee, flexed her fingers and lost herself in her work.

TWENTY-THREE

Twelve hours later, Kay lowered the hairdryer, her senses alert, and then dropped it to the duvet and lunged for her mobile phone as the ringing reached her ears, an unknown number displayed on the screen.

'Hello?'

Silence met her response.

It was all very well handing out her business cards during an investigation but it sometimes meant a less than savoury character found her number, and she held her breath. The banter over a fish and chip supper she'd shared with her team at the end of a long day became a distant memory as she waited for an onslaught of abuse down the line.

'Kay?'

She fumbled the phone in shock, saving it from

dropping to the floor before placing it to her ear, her heart thumping.

'Mum?' Sitting on the bed, she ran a hand through her still-damp hair, her brow furrowed. 'What's wrong?'

'Nothing. I mean, well, your father's still here. In hospital, I mean.'

'Are you all right? Is Dad okay?'

A shaking sigh and the creak of a chair reached her.

'Mum—'

'Don't say anything, Kay. Let me talk.'

A moment passed in which Kay wondered if her mother was still on the end of the call, and then her mother sniffed.

'I've been talking to your father a lot since the weekend,' she said. 'We argued. When I found out you and Adam had left, that summed up everything I thought about you two. That your lives, your jobs, are more important than us. I told your father as much. I didn't want you coming to the hospital anymore, Kay. I couldn't understand why you came all this way at the weekend – I was sure I'd hear about it from Abby afterwards; that you'd sacrificed your job, that Adam's business was suffering.'

She paused, a deep shuddering breath replacing

the vitriol that spewed from her lips, and Kay closed her eyes.

Give her a hardened criminal any day, give her another Mark Sutton; anyone other than the woman who sat in a hospital corridor over a hundred miles away, who hated every ounce of Kay's chosen career.

'Mum—'

'Your father told me to shut up.'

'Pardon?' Kay blinked. 'Did he?'

'Mmm. In hindsight, he probably should've said it more often in the past.' Her mother let out a bitter laugh. 'I suppose it's all too late now. I've always hated your job, Kay – I still do. I hate the danger you put yourself in. I hate not knowing if Adam is going to call us late one night to tell us that you've died, chasing a criminal because you won't let go. You won't give up until you've got the justice you think those victims deserve. And when it killed my granddaughter and you didn't tell me for over a year, I—'

Kay heard the sound of her mother's mobile phone being covered before muffled voices continued a conversation in the background. She tried to make out the words, but gave up in frustration and lay back on the duvet, staring at the ceiling.

'Are you still there?' her mother's voice

squawked.

'I'm here.'

'Good. So, Kay – I need to apologise.'

'W-what?'

'I'm sorry. I'm sorry that I've been so bloody awful to you. And to Adam. I can see how much you two love each other, and he is good for you, I can tell.'

Kay frowned. 'Mum, you're scaring me. What's brought this on? Is Dad going to be okay?'

A moment's silence met her question before her mother recovered.

'Of course he is. He always is, isn't he? Nothing to worry about.'

'Then why—'

'Because what if next time he isn't?' said her mother, her voice dropping to an agonised whisper. 'What happens then? He's the only connection to you I've had.'

'Mum, I'd hate to say it but that's been your choice. You haven't made it easy for us, have you?'

'I know. That's what I've been trying to say. I'm sorry. I want to make amends.'

Kay ran a hand over tired eyes and pushed herself up off the bed before padding across to the dressing table. She tugged a hairbrush through her damp strands of hair and glared at her reflection, her jaw set.

'I'm not going to beg, Kay. Forgive me. Let's put the past behind us. For your father, at least.'

'For Dad? What about you?'

'For me, as well. I want to make a fresh start. Can we do that?'

Kay dropped the hairbrush to the walnut surface with a clatter, and sighed. 'We could try, I suppose.'

'That's good.'

'Why don't you tell me what the doctor said about Dad today? I'm presuming he's not allowed to take calls in the ward?'

'Not yet, no.'

As Kay listened to the update about her father's health, the realisation dawned on her that it was from her mother that she'd inherited her knack for recalling details and complicated terminology. The thought stunned her for a moment, and she sat on the edge of the bed staring into space.

'Kay? Are you still there?'

'Yes. I'm here. So, all's well?'

'It is. Look, maybe when your father gets home and is fit enough, you and Adam could come around here for a Sunday roast? He'd like that, wouldn't he?'

Kay smiled. 'Yes, he would. And so would I.'

TWENTY-FOUR

Kay pulled her woollen gloves from her hands, shoved them into her bag and entered the busy reception area of the town police station.

It was only half past seven in the morning, but the desk sergeant at reception already wore a harassed expression as Kay pressed her security pass against the inner dock lock, the phone ringing incessantly while the man tried to converse with an elderly woman who was clearly hard of hearing.

She gave him a faint smile, then stepped into the corridor beyond and let the door swing shut behind her before hurrying up the stairs.

Quickly shedding her outer layers of clothing, Kay crossed the incident room to the kettle, flipped the switch and set about arranging four mugs for her and her team of detectives.

Barnes was the first to arrive, cursing at full volume about the state of the traffic and lack of parking near the police station, before he was drowned out by Carys who burst through the door on the heels of Gavin and proclaiming the stationery cupboard had been ransacked by a detective sergeant leading a series of burglary investigations in the room next door.

'Debbie will have a fit when she sees what he's done,' she said, taking a steaming mug of coffee from Kay. 'Thanks, guv.'

'Well you can tell her, I'm not,' said Gavin. 'She's scary when she's pissed off.'

Kay let the banter subside while her colleagues switched on their computers, and then corralled them around her desk.

'Right, I'll do the briefing at eight-thirty so check your emails, get updates from the rest of the team and then we'll make a start,' she said. 'Our focus today is determining whether Damien Brancourt left the country and, if he did, where he is right now. This afternoon, we'll look at any connection between him and the protests last year. What time are interviews with his friends and acquaintances, Carys?'

'Nine-thirty, guv.' Carys smiled. 'I remember what I was like as a student so I figured there was no point asking them to come in any earlier.'

'Fair enough. Did you manage to get hold of Julie Rowe?'

'Yes – she's booked in for eleven forty-five. Here's the complete list. Is there anyone else on there that you'd like to speak to?'

Kay ran her gaze down the names and brief summaries Carys and Debbie had collated over the weekend, and then stabbed her finger on the page. 'This one's new. Shaun Browning. It says here he's known Damien since they were at grammar school together.'

'Hughes arranged the interview after speaking with one of Damien's other friends,' said Carys. 'He's due in at three o'clock – does that fit in with your plans?'

'Yes, should be fine, thanks.'

Kay handed back the paperwork before running her eye down a list of actions from the HOLMES database that were displayed on her screen, all gleaned from entries made by the investigative team as they worked and then prioritised by the software's algorithms to assist her with the management of the inquiry.

She checked her watch. 'Too early to expect a phone call from the Border Agency, Gav. What about that CCTV footage?'

'I chased up my contact at Heathrow half an hour ago – he'd just started his shift,' said the detective constable. 'He's going to upload it directly to a secure file transfer protocol site Andy Grey's provided him with. That way, Andy and his team can make a start as soon as it comes through. I'll get a message from Andy when he's got it and I'll log that in the system.'

'Thanks. Let me know as soon as Andy has any news about Damien. Ian – how's your contact in the British Consulate over in Nepal coming along?'

'I got an email from him this morning saying he's waiting for confirmation from the airport in Kathmandu, but—' Barnes broke off as his phone rang. 'Hello?'

Kay resisted the urge to pace the floor as he spoke into the receiver, knowing from experience that a lead could come from anywhere, at any time. There was never a set way an investigation would unfold, and interruptions were a constant expectation.

The older detective replaced the handset and jerked his thumb over his shoulder towards the door. 'That was Simon on the desk downstairs. Amanda Miller is here – the financial investigator from HQ.'

'We'll use Sharp's old office. Do you want to go and get her?'

'Back in a minute. Oh, and like I was saying – nothing from Nepal yet.'

Kay acknowledged the update, and then buttoned her suit jacket and entered the DCI's old office.

Thankfully the cleaners had been in the previous week before the investigation had begun in earnest, so the thin layer of dust she'd spotted on the desk and filing cabinets had been swept away, the remnants of Sharp's presence tidied into neat piles of folders and investigative manuals to one side of a dormant computer.

Kay pulled a threadbare visitor's chair away from the desk and shoved it under the window before substituting it for a different, more comfortable one and then tried not to pace the room while she waited.

The carpet was already worn from Sharp's days of leading investigations from the small police station, and given the budget cuts sweeping the police service, she didn't think a replacement would be installed any time soon.

A polite cough from Barnes preceded a short brunette woman in her mid-fifties entering the office, her face set in a determined expression and a battered leather briefcase in one hand.

Kay held out her hand. 'Amanda Miller?'

'That's me. Good to meet you, DI Hunter.'

'Please, call me Kay. Would you like tea or coffee?' Kay gestured to the visitor's chairs as Barnes followed Amanda into the room and closed the door.

'I'm fine, thanks.'

'Okay.' Kay took Sharp's old seat and rested her hands on the worn ink blotter the DCI had insisted on using. 'I'll be completely honest with you, Amanda. I haven't worked with a financial investigator before, so what do you need from me?'

The woman's lips creased into a smile. 'Well, why don't I begin by telling you what I do, and then we'll devise a plan for your particular problem?'

TWENTY-FIVE

Amanda Miller opened her briefcase and handed Kay and Barnes a slim bound document each.

'When DS Barnes contacted me at the end of last week, the first thing I did was ask for an overview of your investigation to date, together with the matters that give you cause for concern as far as my expertise can help you,' she said. 'Based on that, I've drawn up a scope of work that will act as a guide for my contribution – we can discuss that now, and this is your opportunity to make any amendments to that scope so that we all have a clear understanding of what you need me to do. Does that sound okay?'

Kay nodded, flipping through the pages before her. 'Yes. So, given what you've read so far about our dealings with Sutton Site Security and the allegations against them, what do you suggest we do next?'

Amanda placed her briefcase on the floor beside her chair and crossed her legs. 'I'll be using our ELMER database to start off with. That's what we log all Suspicious Activity Reports into – it helps to build up a story about a company or person over time, and keeps all the information in one place for ease of reference, very similar I suppose to your HOLMES system. The SARs are provided by the financial industry – banks, pension companies, et cetera. Using ELMER, I'll be looking for any evidence of unexplained wealth, unusual cash deposits or pay-outs, that sort of thing. I have access to account numbers, bank statements, pensions, mortgages – everything. We'll soon find out if Mark Sutton's income from his security business is sufficient to support his lifestyle.'

'How does that help us?' said Barnes. 'I mean, we're trying to find out if he had anything to do with the death of Damien Brancourt, not whether he paid his taxes last year.'

Amanda smiled. 'I realise that. This first stage of my work is to build a profile about Sutton, so we can see what we're dealing with. Once I have that, we can start to analyse his accounts and pull apart his business at a micro level. For example, does he have more staff on his various contracts than he claims to be paying? That would indicate he's paying them in cash – now, to me that says two things. He's either dodging tax, or he's using the cash he pays to off-the-books employees to launder money coming into the business. Another example – you stated in your email to me, Ian, that you'd received allegations against Mark Sutton that he'd threatened a construction company in order to win work and had stolen two generators and equipment from them to coerce them into awarding that work to him. You also stated that when you attended Sutton's offices last week, there were no plant vehicles near the building. So, how did he steal the equipment? Did he hire vehicles to remove it from Brancourt and Sons' yard? If he did, how did he pay for it? Can we find evidence that way? Do you see what I mean?'

'Got you,' said Barnes. 'What about the people who work for him? I can't imagine Mark Sutton would dirty his hands – he'd get someone else to steal the equipment for him and carry out any threats on site.'

'Well, there's always the use of cash machines and tying that in to any CCTV footage you can get,' said Amanda. 'Once I've delved into the banking records for the company I can ascertain what debit cards have been issued to Sutton and his staff. I can also see if those cards have been used anywhere near Brancourt's premises, home or work sites. I'll put together a comprehensive map of the area showing the usage for each card and we can go from there. Does that sound good to you?'

Kay sat back in her chair, her excitement building. 'It does, yes. What do you need from us at this stage?'

'I've already got clearance from HQ for the HOLMES records relating to this investigation,' said Amanda. 'The best way to do this – and I'm speaking from experience – is to let me have a couple of days to flush out the final details I need about Sutton Site Security from the SARs on file and your interviews to date, and then I'll provide you with an interim report in a few days to let you know where I'm up to and the steps I believe we need to follow after that. Don't worry,' she added, seeing the look of horror that crossed Barnes's face, 'there won't be lots of paperwork for you to wade through; I appreciate you've got other angles of this investigation to follow. Think of it more as a checklist – a way for you to ensure our two investigations are complementing each other. It also gives you the opportunity to steer me towards any other matters you've found that you want me to take a look at.'

Kay turned to a fresh page of her notebook and jotted down the agreed action plan. 'That sounds good. Is there anything else we should be aware of?'

'Yes. I must insist that until my investigation is concluded we keep my involvement confidential. We can't afford to let anyone at Sutton Site Security know that we're doing this. At present, it's only a desktop study but if I can find something you can use as leverage against them in relation to your case, I'll let you know immediately.'

Kay rose from her seat and held out her hand. 'This is a thorough scope, thank you. We've got a desk for you in the incident room ready and waiting. Barnes – could you show Amanda where to find everything out there, and then we'll catch up?'

'Guv.'

The older detective showed Amanda to the door, and as they disappeared from sight Kay wandered over to the window and let her gaze drift across the car park below.

The financial investigator's enthusiasm was infectious; Kay could feel the excitement clutching at her chest.

Surely they would find something they could use against Mark Sutton?

What if he had threatened Damien Brancourt in order to coerce his father into awarding the contract? Had Damien somehow discovered about the fraudulent contract award and confronted Sutton?

She turned at the sound of footsteps.

Barnes closed the door and raised an eyebrow. 'Bloody hell, Kay – she's good.'

'I hope so, Ian. We haven't got much else to go on at the moment.'

TWENTY-SIX

Kay stabbed the code into the keypad on the door to interview room two with her forefinger and stepped over the threshold, closing the door before crossing to the table at the far end of the room.

Carys sat on one side of it, her notebook open to a fresh page.

As Kay approached, she took in the sight of the slim woman sitting opposite the detective constable.

Julie Rowe picked at the skin on her thumbnail, her brown hair pulled into a severe top knot that did nothing for her appearance. Her mouth wore a petulant expression as she raised her gaze to Kay.

'Julie Rowe? Thanks for coming in,' she said.

'Didn't have much of a choice, did I?'

Kay ignored the remark and instead turned to Carys. 'Shall we make a start?'

Carys nodded, then recited the standard caution for a witness interview. That done, she opened the folder.

'Julie, can you begin by telling us how you know Damien Brancourt?'

Kay silently congratulated her younger protégée. At present, they were working on the basis that the Brancourts' insistence that the body found in the ceiling of the Petersham Building wasn't Damien, and Carys had chosen to interview each of his friends and acquaintances accordingly. No mention of the possibility that Damien Brancourt had met his death on his father's construction site was to be made during the discussions.

'Uni. A few years ago.'

'Were you studying the same subjects?' said Carys.

'God, no.' Julie choked out a laugh. 'He was studying business, project management – stuff like that. I was finishing a master's degree in politics.'

'Are you older than him?'

'By about a year and a half, yeah. We got talking in the student union bar one night. He was working there to earn a bit of extra money.'

'It's a long way from having a drink to staging a protest,' said Carys. 'How'd you get involved with that?'

Julie shrugged, her gaze dropping to her hands. 'Seems stupid now, looking back.'

'Go on.'

'Well, we just wanted to make a point, y'know? There's better things for the council to be spending money on around here than doing up old buildings.'

'Who organised the protests?'

'I did.' Julie shuffled in her seat and sat up straighter. 'I knew that if I didn't, they'd never happen. Everyone else – including Damien – were talkers, not doers.'

'How did you convince Damien Brancourt to get involved, given that his father was one of the construction managers for the redevelop projects?'

A faint smile crossed Julie's lips. 'I think he and his dad had had a disagreement of some sort a few days before. I think it was Damien's way of sticking two fingers up at his parents, that's all.' Her face clouded. 'Hey, he's not in trouble is he? Damien, I mean.'

'When was the last time you saw him?' said Kay.

The woman exhaled as she gazed at the ceiling.

'Um, I guess it must've been June. Yeah. Before it got really hot.'

'Did he say what his plans were for the summer?'

'Yeah. Lucky bugger was going travelling. Nepal, I think.'

'How close were you with Damien before he left?' said Carys.

'We weren't sleeping together, if that's what you mean,' said Julie, wrinkling her nose. 'Not my type. Bit posh, to be honest. Have you seen his parents' house? It's massive.'

'You've been there?'

Julie shook her head. 'Not inside – I had to drop him off there after one of our demonstrations.'

'He didn't drive?'

'Said he didn't want a car. Probably because he was off travelling – no point having one and it sitting on the driveway for nearly a year, right?'

'Tell us about the incident at the protest,' said Kay. 'Damien was arrested for an altercation with one of the security guards.'

'Bloody idiot. I told all of them that it was meant to be a peaceful protest, but Damien didn't listen. I don't know what started it – I only heard the bloke shout after Damien went for him, but afterwards when

I asked, Damien said the man had insulted his dad, so he punched him.'

Carys flipped through her notes. 'That was the security guard, Jeff Donovan?'

'I don't know his name. He was wearing one of those uniforms with the three S's embroidered on the front of it – over his heart.'

'Did you speak to Damien after he was released?'

'Only briefly.' Julie sighed and leaned back in her seat. 'I told him I didn't want him to come to any more demonstrations if he couldn't keep his temper under control. I don't need that sort of trouble on my record.'

'Your record?' said Carys.

Julie's features brightened. 'Yes. I'm planning to run for Parliament one day. Represent local interests on a national level.'

'Were you or Damien ever threatened during or after the protest?' said Kay.

The woman shook her head. 'No. That's the thing. The only person who threatened anyone was Damien when he went after that bloke. I heard him say it.'

'Say what?'

'That if he and his boss didn't leave Damien's dad alone, they'd regret it.'

TWENTY-SEVEN

Kay leaned against the plasterwork of the corridor from the interview suite and watched as Carys led Julie Rowe back through the doors to the reception area.

The woman's witness statement troubled her.

She'd read the formal documentation following Damien Brancourt's arrest, and no formal complaint had been made against him in relation to the alleged threats he'd made towards Jeffrey Donovan, the security guard.

They only had Julie's assertion that there was more to the scuffle than a student protest.

What had Damien been up to? What had he been trying to achieve?

Kay pushed herself away from the wall as Carys

reappeared, wearing a perplexed expression that Kay was sure matched her own.

'What do you think, guv?' she said.

'Have any of his other friends mentioned anything about threats towards Sutton Site Security?'

'I haven't heard anything yet, but Gavin and Parker should be completing the last of the interviews in about half an hour.'

'All right. We'll have an early briefing to go over the highlights rather than wait for all the information to be updated into HOLMES. Why don't you take a break and get yourself some lunch? You've been going nonstop since this time last week.'

'Thanks, guv. I've got to admit, I'm starving.'

Kay jerked her thumb over her shoulder. 'I'm going to grab a seat in the observation suite. See if I can learn anything from this interview before it ends. Could you get me a sandwich or something?'

'Will do. See you in a bit.'

Carys hurried away and Kay walked along the corridor until she reached a solid door with a security warning on a sign pinned to its surface.

She swiped her security card across the locking mechanism to one side, then entered the room.

A series of computer screens were placed on a

long fitted wooden desk opposite the door, two of which were on.

Kay pulled up a chair in front of them and sank into it with a sigh, then reached out and turned up the volume control under one of the displays.

On screen, Gavin and Parker were sitting on one side of a desk facing a man in his twenties who ran a hand through a dark fringe damp with sweat.

Kay flipped open her notebook until she found a note of the man's name.

Shaun Browning.

The team's research showed that Browning had been at grammar school with Damien Brancourt, eventually securing a place at the University of Winchester.

Right now, he looked as if he'd much rather be back in Hampshire rather than sitting in a dingy interview room at a Kentish police station.

'When was the last time you saw Damien?' said Gavin, his voice containing a metallic edge due to the way the microphones had been set up in the room.

'In April,' said Browning. 'We don't socialise much these days, but someone we knew at school got engaged and we were both invited to the party.'

'Whose engagement?' said Gavin.

'Ian Marlow.'

Parker thrust a pen and paper across the desk. 'We'll need his details, please. Address and phone number.'

Browning obliged, and Kay narrowed her eyes at the screen.

The man's hand shook as he scrawled across the page, and he dropped the pen when he was finished as if it burned his fingers.

'What did you discuss with Damien?' said Parker.

'Christ, I can't remember. It was seven or eight months ago. I know he was planning to go travelling in Nepal. He mentioned that.'

'How did he seem when you last saw him? Did he say or do anything that gave you cause for concern?' said Gavin.

Browning's head jerked as he turned to face the detective constable, his features turning pink. 'Like what? Is he in trouble or something?'

'Answer the question, please.'

'No, he was just Damien. Same as always. Chip on his shoulder about something or other and happy to complain about it to anyone who would listen. I got tired of it after ten minutes and made my excuses. Ended up chatting with a girl from Paddock Wood.' He sat back in his seat, his shoulders relaxing a little. 'Getting married to her next year, actually.'

'Congratulations.'

Kay snorted at Gavin's tone; it was evident the detective was frustrated with the lack of progress in the interview and after another twenty minutes of questioning, it seemed that Shaun Browning was going to be of no further use to the investigation.

Gavin terminated the interview and switched off the recording equipment, although he left the man sitting at the desk when he exited the room with Parker.

Kay pushed her way out into the corridor and met them as they were walking towards the exit.

'How come Shaun Browning looked so nervous when you were interviewing him?' she said.

Parker grinned. 'Uniform picked him up this morning before we got a chance to contact him,' he said. 'Found a small amount of cannabis on him.'

Kay rolled her eyes. 'Great. Did you charge him?'

Parker shook his head. 'We'll let him off with a caution. He's got an interview tomorrow with one of the big manufacturing companies over at Aylesford. Didn't think it was worth spoiling his week, given it's a first time offence.'

'He won't get the job anyway if he doesn't pass the drug and alcohol test that company insists upon,' Gavin said, a grin on his face. 'Idiot. Thought we'd leave him in there to stew for a bit before getting someone to show him the way out.'

'No further information about this grudge that Damien Brancourt had?'

'Not so much a grudge,' said Parker, turning a page in his notebook and peering at his writing. 'Apparently John Brancourt has always expected Damien to take over the business and Damien doesn't want to. Thinks it's below him.'

'Families, eh?' said Kay. 'All right, go and read him the riot act about the cannabis and then I'll see you back upstairs. Briefing in half an hour.'

'Guv.'

KAY BRUSHED crumbs from her suit trousers and scrunched up the paper bag as she licked the last of the butter from her fingertips.

Snatching a paper tissue from the box she shared with Barnes, she wiped her hands then tossed the rubbish into the bin under her desk and locked her computer screen.

'Right, everyone. Front of the room,' she called, pushing back her chair. 'Carys, can you let us have an overview of the other interviews conducted today?'

The detective constable weaved her way to the front of the room before addressing her colleagues.

'We've interviewed eight witnesses since this morning, and apart from Julie Rowe and Shaun Browning no-one has a bad word to say about Damien Brancourt. Three of them hadn't kept in contact with him since leaving university, one had worked with him briefly at the petrol station on the A20 when they were in sixth form school, and the other four were at university with him until last year. None of them were close to him – they followed each other on social media, but that's about it. On that point, we did question them whether they'd seen any posts from Damien while he's been in Nepal but they hadn't – all of them stated that they believed the reason for this was that he doesn't have an internet connection out there.'

'Makes sense. Thank you.' Kay waited until Carys had reached her seat before bringing the team up to date with the interviews of Julie Rowe and Shaun Browning. She tapped her finger on their photos pinned to the whiteboard. 'All right, what do we think? Anyone?'

'What if Damien's threat towards Jeff Donovan was taken seriously by Mark Sutton, who decided to hand out his own form of retribution?' said Gavin.

'Sort of a tit for tat gone wrong you mean?' said Barnes.

'Yes. Maybe they meant to rough him up a bit, but it went too far.'

Kay frowned and turned away from the whiteboard, twirling the pen between her fingers. 'Could be, except we know from Lucas that Damien – presuming it's him – was electrocuted before he suffered the head wound. Get Donovan in for questioning first thing in the morning. I'll be interested to hear what he's got to say about Damien and their altercation.'

'Do you think he was tortured, guv?' said Carys. 'With electrocution, I mean.'

A shocked silence replaced the muted conversations taking place around the incident room as her words sank in.

'Bloody hell,' said Barnes.

Kay's gaze fell to the carpet for a moment as she mulled over her response. 'Carys – can you get onto Lucas straight after this briefing and ask him to review his post mortem report in light of your theory? See if he can find anything to support it.'

'Will do, guv.'

'If our victim was tortured, then Mark Sutton is a lot more dangerous than we've realised. From now on, I want you working in pairs outside of this room, is that understood?'

'Guv.'

'Yes, guv.'

'And no-one, I repeat *no-one* goes anywhere near Mark Sutton unless myself or Barnes is with you. That's an order.'

TWENTY-EIGHT

Kay hovered at Gavin's shoulder and stared through the privacy glass at the man sitting in interview room one, before narrowing her eyes.

'He's expecting the worst if he's got Brian Sutherland representing him,' she muttered.

'Good, is he?' said Gavin, sliding a clean notebook across the desk to Barnes.

'Patient. Needs to be, with some of the people he hangs around with. You ready, Ian?'

'Guv.' Barnes snatched up the notebook, pocketed a pen and then led the way out of the door and through to the interview room.

He started the recording, provided the necessary caution to Jeffrey Donovan and introduced those present, before gesturing to Kay.

'Let's start with your employment at Sutton Site Security, Mr Donovan,' said Kay, ignoring the solicitor who rolled his eyes and uncapped his fountain pen.

'What about it?'

'How long have you worked for Mark Sutton?'

'Since I got out of prison four years ago.'

'And how did you apply?'

'Apply?'

'How did you get the job?'

'I've known Mark for a few years,' said Donovan. 'I used to drive a taxi. When I stopped doing that, he offered me a job.'

'Why did you stop driving a taxi?'

'What's that got to do with your investigation, detective?' said Sutherland, raising an eyebrow.

'Context,' she said, and then turned back to his client. 'Answer the question, Jeffrey.'

Donovan glanced at his solicitor, who gave a slight shrug.

'I lost my licence.'

'Why?'

'Got caught drink driving.' He smirked. 'They banned me for twelve months, so I needed money 'cause I couldn't work. Mark gave me a job and when

I got my licence back I decided I didn't fancy driving the taxi anymore so I stayed with him.'

Kay opened the file that Barnes handed to her. 'Do you hold any formal security qualifications?'

'No. I don't need them. I don't work in any licensed premises, and it's not like I'm guarding any kids, is it?'

'So what qualifies you to work for Mark Sutton's security business?'

His top lip curled. 'Experience.'

'Tell me about Damien Brancourt.'

'What about him?'

'Why did he punch you?'

'You'll have to ask him. I don't know.'

'A witness we've spoken to says that Damien Brancourt told you and Mark Sutton to leave his dad alone.'

Donovan blinked, but remained silent.

'Furthermore, our witness states that Damien implied there would be consequences if you didn't heed his warning.' Kay folded her hands and stared at Donovan. 'What's your involvement with John Brancourt?'

Donovan crossed his arms over his chest, and then sat back in his seat. 'I worked on one of his sites.

Through Mark. Security and the like. Except he decided he wasn't going to pay on time.'

'What did you do?'

'Me? I didn't do nothing. Mark paid me no matter what happens between him and his clients. Makes no difference to me if Brancourt don't pay his bills.'

'What did Mark do?'

Donovan held up his hands. 'How should I know? First thing I knew about it is when his boy spotted me, dropped the sign he'd been waving in the air and came after me.'

Kay turned at a knock on the door. 'Come in.'

Carys appeared, a note between her fingers. She handed it to Kay before turning on her heel, closing the door behind her.

Kay looked over at Donovan. 'Interesting. It appears that you're no longer employed by Mark Sutton. Since when?'

'About May. Yeah, May. Before it got hot.'

'Why not?'

'I don't know. I suppose the work dried up.'

'Where do you work now?'

'Here and there. I do a couple of days pulling pints at one of the pubs in town.'

'Why didn't you press charges against Damien Brancourt?' Kay flicked through the pages in the file.

'You didn't even respond to my colleagues' phone calls to come in and let them have a statement about the assault.'

'No need was there? I mean, the boy was an idiot, but no harm done. I think your lot made more out of it than it was, to be honest. More trouble than it was worth for me to get involved.'

Kay slipped a photograph of the mummified body at the crime scene across the table to Donovan. 'We've reason to believe this is what remains of Damien Brancourt. The victim was found in the ceiling cavity of another building Sutton Site Security was guarding. That contract had been awarded to Mark Sutton by John Brancourt under dubious circumstances.'

Donovan tore his eyes away from the photograph. 'So?'

'Did you kill Damien Brancourt and hide his body?'

'No!' Spittle covered the man's lips. 'I never killed no-one. You said it yourself – I haven't worked for Mark since May, so I couldn't have done that, could I?'

Brian Sutherland put a restraining hand on his client's arm, and then glared at Kay. 'Explain yourself, Detective Hunter. My client takes offence at such accusations.'

Kay waited until Donovan had settled. 'Then explain to me why Damien threatened you only months before his death. And why you seem to know that Damien disappeared in June.'

'I told you, I've got no idea about the threat. It seemed to come out of the blue. Probably only targeted me because he could see the logo on my shirt. It could've happened to any of us.' He shrugged. 'And it must've been someone else who works for Mark who told me Damien wasn't around in June. He was going on holiday or something, wasn't he?'

'Working for charity in Nepal, actually.'

Donovan's face broke into a wicked smile. 'Charity work, my arse. Little runt was running away from his responsibilities, wasn't he? Didn't want to work for his old man. What's the point in taking over a business that's dying a death?'

TWENTY-NINE

Kay fought down the familiar sensation of impatience as she watched the team of detectives and uniformed officers assemble in the incident room the next morning.

Finally, after days of speculation and second-guessing her decisions, it seemed they had a breakthrough that would enable them to focus their attention on narrowing a field of suspects.

The youngest police constable in the team had only sunk into a seat in the middle of the small crowd when Kay began.

'Gavin – perhaps you could bring our colleagues up to speed with what we've learned this morning.'

'Guv.' Gavin rose from his chair and nodded to two administrative staff who parted ways to let him through, eventually positioning himself at the side of the room next to the window. He waited until the murmur of voices had dissipated, then closed his notebook.

'I received an email overnight from the British Consulate in Kathmandu. They have no record of Damien Brancourt contacting them in distress for any matter, nor do they have a note of his ever arriving in the country.'

The hubbub of voices began once more, the excitement palpable.

Gavin held up his hand to silence his colleagues. 'We've also received a phone call this morning from the UK Border Agency. Damien Brancourt hasn't used his passport since a week-long trip to Magaluf two and a half years ago.'

The incident room exploded with chatter.

'Thanks, Gavin.' Kay raised her voice over that of her colleagues. 'All right, pipe down everyone. Barnes – you're next.'

'Guv.' Barnes pushed himself away from the wall he'd been leaning against. 'I've spoken with Andy Grey, and he confirms his team have concluded viewing the CCTV footage from major London train stations and Heathrow airport – all five terminals. There's been no sighting of Damien Brancourt in any of the images, either inside or outside. Andy confirmed he had them check twelve hours either side of Damien's flight to make sure. He never showed up.'

'All right,' said Kay. 'Next steps. Amanda – I wonder if we could draw on your expertise and find out if Damien used his ATM card anywhere in the twenty-four hours leading up to his death? I want to wait until we have the results from the DNA test Lucas is running against the sample given to us by John Brancourt before we go back to the parents with the news so let's use this time to trace Damien's last movements locally. It's quite clear he never made it to Heathrow, so sometime after having dinner at his parents' house that night and John dropping him off at Maidstone East station, Damien went to the Petersham Building, where he subsequently died.'

'Will do,' said Amanda. 'I'll go back a week in the timeline as well, so that I can get a feel for his movements in the days leading up to his death.'

Barnes pulled out his notebook. 'What about Mark Sutton?'

'Leave him for a moment. I want to find out what happened to Damien before we speak to him again. I don't fancy interviewing him when I've only got half the information we need.'

Barnes nodded, then lowered his head and updated his notes.

Kay turned to the uniformed officers who comprised over half her investigative team. 'We'll reconvene in six hours. I want a full picture of where Damien Brancourt was the day he supposedly left for the airport. Work every angle you can, speak to your colleagues who police the town centre on a regular basis and get onto that local CCTV footage. Someone out there knows what happened to him.'

The incident room filled with the sound of chairs scuffing across carpet as the team dispersed, and Kay exhaled.

At some point, she would have to speak to Damien Brancourt's parents again, but until she had conclusive evidence it was indeed their son who had been discovered in the ceiling cavity of the Petersham Building, she had to wait for Lucas Anderson's findings to support her conviction.

However long it took.

KAY TOOK the cardboard tray from the assistant behind the counter of the café and elbowed her way out of the door, a chill gust of wind from the river blowing up Earl Street and making her gasp.

She balanced the two takeout cups of coffee in one hand and shoved the other in the pocket of her wool coat, wishing she'd remembered to wear the scarf that was currently folded up in her desk drawer.

Increasing her pace, she reached the bottom of the road and turned left towards the Archbishop's Palace.

While the team had taken it in turns to rush out and find something to eat for lunch, Barnes had sidled up to her desk and asked if she'd meet him at their usual place for a chat.

She'd agreed readily, noticing her colleague's reticence and mindful of the advice she'd given to her team to get some fresh air.

She simply hadn't banked on that air being quite so fresh.

A shiver wracked her as she stood at the pedestrian crossing waiting for the light opposite to flash green and then she hurried across, casting an eye over the congested traffic that wrapped its way between College Road and Fairmeadow.

She found Barnes on the bench behind the Archbishop's Palace, hunkered in his thick coat while he glared at the river as if it held sole responsibility for the cold snap that gripped the county town.

'Here. Two sugars.'

'Thanks.'

He slid along the bench to make room for her, wrapping his fingers around the takeout coffee cup.

After a few minutes' silence while they watched a tourist boat slip from its moorings before its pilot steered it downstream, Kay turned to her colleague.

'All right. What's up? You're not normally this quiet.'

A quirk twitched at the corner of his mouth. 'Make the most of it.'

Kay remained silent, waiting for him to gather his thoughts.

Eventually, Barnes spoke. 'I'm worried I don't have the support of the team, Kay.'

'What?'

'I mean, when you're not there. I wonder if they trust me like they trust you.' His voice cracked, and he glanced away from her. 'I wonder if they respect me, and then I worry that they don't, and that it'll affect this investigation – and others.'

Kay rocked back on the bench, stunned. 'Barnes, I can assure you that everyone back in that incident room has your back. So do I, and Sharp. He was only telling me last week how pleased he was you took on the role of detective sergeant. I can't imagine working with anyone else.'

'It's just… I'm starting to question my own capabilities, you know? I forgot how much you had to juggle in this role. I'm scared I'll let you down, Kay.'

She sniffed, then rose from the seat, dusted down the back of her coat and lobbed the empty coffee cup into the bin nearby before turning back to Barnes.

'You've never let me down, Ian. And I don't believe you're going to start now. I know taking on this role was a big decision for you, but trust me – there's nobody else I'd want in my corner. You're like the glue in this team.'

Barnes lowered his gaze. 'Thanks.'

'You're going to have days like this when you question every decision you make, and you'll wonder if you're out of your depth, but that's when you look around you. See who in the team has the skills and strengths you feel you need, and you delegate.' She smiled. 'And it *is* bloody hard work, juggling all of that.'

He exhaled, then straightened. 'Thank you. Sometimes I watch you, and you make it look so easy that I forget what you've been through to get where you are.'

'I couldn't do it without you.' She leaned over and

mock punched him on his shoulder. 'Come on. Back in the saddle.'

Barnes stood, brushing off the back of his wool coat and dropped his takeout coffee cup into the waste bin beside the bench before following her up the winding path beside the Archbishop's Palace.

Kay smiled as he hurried to catch up and then fell into step beside her.

'Well that pep talk seems to have put a spring in your stride.'

'Don't take this the wrong way, guv. It's not because of your management style. I can't wait to get back indoors – it's bloody freezing out here.'

THIRTY

'We've got Damien Brancourt on CCTV the afternoon he was meant to be travelling to Nepal,' said Gavin.

Kay dropped her coat over the back of her chair and hurried over to where he sat with two uniformed constables, their eyes fixed to the computer screens before them.

'And we've got a pattern of ATM usage,' said Amanda. She crossed the room and held out a sheaf of paperwork to Kay, giving a copy to Gavin. 'Small amounts, twenty pounds most of the time but then two hundred pounds on the morning of his death.'

'Holiday spending money?' said Kay. She flipped the page, running her gaze down the list of transactions.

'That's what I'm thinking,' said Amanda. 'But that last transaction was made at ten thirty-two in the morning.'

'And the Petersham Building was full of contractors then, so he must've gone back there in the evening.'

'That's what we're looking at here, guv,' said Gavin.

One of the uniformed officers sprang from his seat and gestured to Kay to take his place.

'Thanks,' she said. 'Let's see it, then.'

The constable next to her operated the controls and hit the "pause" button as a shadowy figure came into view.

'This is the ATM on the corner where Rose Yard comes out on the High Street. It's the one he used that morning. He walks straight past it this time.'

'And he's carrying no luggage. A bit strange for someone who's meant to be catching a flight that night,' said Kay.

'He looks happy enough,' said Barnes. 'Not like he's about to do a midnight flit or is running away from something or someone.'

'We lose him here when he turns into Wyke Manor Road,' said the constable.

'Isn't there any CCTV coverage up that street?'

'Not back then, but given the council's focus had been on the redevelopment works, replacing it might have been at the bottom of their "to do" list,' said Gavin. 'I checked this morning with them – the camera was up and running by the end of July.'

'And maybe none of the development companies contracted by the council were worried, given a lot of them had their own security measures in place,' said Barnes. He leaned over Kay's shoulder and tapped the screen. 'Damien could have cut behind these buildings from this street and reached the Petersham Building that way. If we're going to speak to Mark Sutton again, we can put it to him that Damien Brancourt has been seen in the vicinity of the area he was contracted to secure and see what his reaction is.'

Kay pushed back the chair and thanked the two constables before leading Barnes and Gavin towards the whiteboard. She peered up at the photographs that had been collated since the start of the investigation and resisted the urge to sigh.

Instead, she waved Carys over to join them. 'Okay, Julie Rowe reckons she overheard Damien threatening one of Sutton's men at the protest and a scuffle ensued, resulting in Damien's arrest. Sutton's employee didn't press charges, so he was subsequently let off with a caution. A few months later, Damien's hours away from leaving the country for a planned trip to Nepal but decides to divert back into Maidstone that night instead. Did you see the time stamp on the camera footage? It's after Annabelle Brancourt said they'd had dinner together, and John had taken him to the train station by then. So, where the hell is Damien's suitcase – or a bag?'

Three perplexed faces stared back at her.

'John never mentioned Damien making a detour into the town centre when we spoke to him,' said Barnes after a moment.

'Maybe because he knew nothing of it,' said Carys. 'If Damien asked to be dropped off while he ran an errand or something, maybe it wouldn't seem out of character to his dad.'

Kay ran a hand through her hair as she looked at Damien's photograph. 'What the hell were you doing?'

A phone rang on a desk in the far corner of the room, and it was a few seconds before she realised it was her mobile, such was her frustration at the lack of information she stared at.

'Guv?' said Carys. 'Phone?'

'Christ – somebody get that!'

Kay sprinted between the desks as Philip Parker held her phone aloft.

'It's Lucas Anderson, guv.'

'Cheers.' Kay took the phone and put it on speakerphone as the other detectives joined her. 'What have you got for us, Lucas?'

'We've got a match,' said the pathologist. 'John Brancourt's DNA tested positive. The body that was in the ceiling is Damien Brancourt, without a doubt.'

THIRTY-ONE

Barnes pressed the doorbell then took a step back and peered up at the large wrought-iron framed window above the portico of the Brancourts' home.

'Doesn't get any easier, these house calls,' he muttered. 'Especially when we've already done it once.'

Kay didn't respond, her thoughts similar to her colleague's words.

She turned away and cast her eyes over the ornate front garden, the plants wilted in the cold air. Beyond a moss-covered bird bath, a male blackbird pecked at the lawn seeking some form of sustenance.

Lucas had ended his call to her an hour earlier with the news that Damien Brancourt's electrocution hadn't indicated he'd been tortured, much to the whole team's relief.

It still didn't eliminate Mark Sutton from her enquiries, though, and Kay had reiterated her warning to her colleagues that the man should not be approached alone.

Her focus returned to the house as a bolt shot back from the door a second before it was opened.

Annabelle Brancourt frowned when she saw them. 'You again?'

'Can we have a word, please?' said Barnes. 'Is your husband in?'

The woman stood to one side and gestured for them to enter. 'He's in the kitchen. Go on through – you know where it is.'

Kay led the way along the hallway, her focus on the floor rather than the luxurious surroundings this time. She knew the Brancourts would never recover from the news she was about to share with them, and the house would no longer feel like a home.

A sadness swept through her, taking her by surprise. She bit her lip to force down the emotion and shoved open the door through to the kitchen, an aroma of garlic and herbs wafting over her.

John Brancourt turned from the sink, a tea towel

and wine glass in his hand. 'Something the matter, Detective Hunter? We were about to have dinner.'

Kay waited until Annabelle had followed Barnes and then moved closer to the table, eyeing the two places set and the bottle of Merlot that appeared to have been opened moments before. 'Are you expecting anyone else?'

'No, it's just us tonight. Christopher and Bethany – the twins – are out,' said Annabelle.

'Oh? How old are they?' said Kay.

'Sixteen,' said Annabelle. 'Look, I'm supposed to be dishing up in fifteen minutes. What is it you want?'

Barnes turned his attention to John. 'When we first spoke with you, you stated you took your son to the train station so he could travel to Heathrow and catch his flight to Nepal last June. Is there anything else you'd like to add to that?'

John lowered his gaze before setting the wine glass down on the worktop and took a seat at the table, his fingers twisting the tea towel. 'I did intend to take Damien to the train station, but when we got nearer to town he asked me to let him out nearby rather than at the station itself. Said he'd arranged to meet a friend and they were going to travel to the airport together.'

Kay pulled out a chair opposite him and leaned forward, her interest piqued. 'Where did you drop him off?'

'At a bus stop on Sittingbourne Road, near the pub on the roundabout.'

'Why didn't you tell me?' Annabelle glared at her husband. 'You said you took him to the train station. You said there weren't any problems.'

'There wasn't a problem.' John sighed and held up his hands. 'Look, I'm sorry. But he was so excited about the trip, and then when he told me about this friend he wanted to meet, I could see I was going to be in the way. Apparently they were going to have a couple of drinks and then wander into town to catch the train.'

'Did he tell you his friend's name?' said Barnes.

'No. I didn't ask, either. I didn't see anything wrong with it.'

Kay sighed and turned to Annabelle. 'Would you like to sit?'

'I'm fine here.' The woman folded her arms across her chest.

'All right. Look, I'm sorry to have to be the bearer of this news. We've had a phone call from our pathologist about an hour ago. The DNA results came back positive. We've double checked everything, including with the British Consulate in Kathmandu. I'm so sorry Annabelle, John. The body discovered in the Petersham Building is confirmed as being Damien. He never caught his flight to Nepal.'

'What? No.' The woman's bottom lip quivered, and then she took a step back as a wail emanated from her, the agony of the news clear in her tear-streaked eyes. She gulped at the air as if struggling to breathe.

John Brancourt collapsed into the chair, his head in his hands. 'What do we do now? Damien…'

Kay pushed away from her seat and crossed the kitchen to where a water filter jug sat next to a kettle and filled two glasses, returning to the table to pass one to John before taking the other to Annabelle.

'Here,' she said. 'Small sips.'

She hovered next to her, watching her carefully as she struggled to control her breathing.

Eventually, Annabelle passed back the glass after a sip and waved her hand at it. 'I've had enough.'

Kay took the water. 'Sit down. Please.'

She waited until Annabelle joined her husband at the table, noting that she didn't sit next to him but choosing instead to perch on the corner of the window seat.

'We've analysed the CCTV footage for all London train stations and the Heathrow terminals,' said Barnes. 'Damien doesn't show up in any of them so based on what you've told us, John, we'll widen the search to include cameras along the Sittingbourne Road as well to see if we can trace Damien's movements and find out who this friend of his was.'

'I don't understand why he hung around,' said John. 'Why didn't he go to Heathrow? Why didn't he phone me? I had my mobile on hands-free. I could've turned around and gone to get him if he was worried about something.'

Kay's heart clenched at the distress in Brancourt's voice.

'We don't know yet, but you have my word we'll find the answers,' she said.

THIRTY-TWO

The next morning, Kay faced her colleagues to bring them up to date with the interview she and Barnes had conducted with Damien Brancourt's parents.

'Gavin – can you take a look at CCTV along the Sittingbourne Road and surrounding area? We need to find this so-called "friend" Damien was meeting, and find out who he is, and what he knows about his death. Make that your priority this morning.'

'Will do, guv.'

'Carys – while he's doing that, get onto uniform and ask for some help to interview the licensees and staff of any of the pubs within a one-mile radius of Damien's drop-off point. Again, we need to get our hands on that information as quickly as possible, so do what you can to expedite it.'

'Guv.'

Kay ran her gaze down the HOLMES report Debbie had printed out for her, checking through the tasks the database had assigned and delegating these to her team. Finally, when the last order had been given, she picked up a sheaf of papers and held it up.

'This is Amanda's initial findings into Sutton Security Services. It's been saved into HOLMES, so have a read of it when you get back to your desks. Amanda – can you provide an overview for everyone?'

The financial investigator pushed back her chair and joined Kay at the front of the room. 'From what we've managed to glean from ELMER, it appears on the surface that Mark Sutton is running a tight ship. There are none of the obvious signs we look for – unexplained large deposits or credits to the business accounts, no tax audits carried out on the business in the eight years it's been trading.'

Barnes leaned his elbows on his knees and emitted a loud sigh. 'So, we've got nothing on him, is that what you're saying?'

Amanda smiled. 'No, quite the opposite. We simply had to delve a little deeper into the system. Detective Hunter, can I use the overhead projector a moment?'

'Of course.' Kay signalled to Parker and stepped to one side while he dragged a small table across the carpet and then set the projector on top of it, pointing it at the blank wall above a filing cabinet. 'Thanks.'

After logging in, Amanda executed a series of commands before a photograph appeared showing a car wash business.

'I know that place,' said Gavin.

'Right, and there are a few locally but this is one we've been keeping our eye on, due to the fact that most of the staff are paid cash in hand. The problem with these roadside car washes is that they're popular amongst people-smuggling gangs up and down the country,' said Amanda. She approached the image, and tapped her finger on a figure lurking in the background, his face in shadow. 'This is Barry Esher, a close associate of Mark Sutton. Mr Esher is a person of interest for my team because he's previously spent time at Her Majesty's pleasure for fraud and extortion.'

'When was he released from prison?' said Kay, her interest piqued.

'A couple of years ago. Since then, and similar to Gary Hudson, he's acted as enforcer for Mark Sutton. Sutton doesn't like to get his hands dirty, that much is evident.'

'How does this help us?' said Carys. 'None of the people we've spoken to about Damien Brancourt have mentioned him ever going near this place.'

'Because Barry Esher is also known as Adrian Sutton. He's Mark Sutton's cousin.' Amid the stunned silence that filled the incident room, Amanda pulled out a page from her file, handing it to Kay. 'He changed his name by deed poll twelve years ago after an altercation in Bromley that left one man dead. Adrian got away with it, but disappeared for a few years. When he came back under his new name, it appeared that he hadn't learned his lesson because he beat up a patron of a pub in Chatham so badly the man lost a kidney. He did time for that as well. What's more, Adrian Sutton signed the security roster to enter the Petersham Building the day Damien Brancourt was supposedly flying to Nepal. He's scrawled his signature on the page so it's hard to recognise, but I've seen it before. It's him.'

Barnes emitted a low whistle. 'Bloody hell, Amanda. Good work.'

'I'll second that,' said Kay, unable to keep the sense of wonder from her voice as she skim-read the report. 'Thank you.'

She waited until Amanda had retaken her seat, and then moved to the whiteboard, pen in hand.

'Okay, next steps. I want Barry Esher – also known as Adrian Sutton – and Gary Hudson brought in for questioning as soon as possible. We're treating them as suspects, so act accordingly. Gavin, can you liaise with uniform to organise that?'

'Guv.'

'Next, Carys – can you take Debbie and Hughes with you and interview the workers at the car wash this morning? I realise you might not get much out of them if they are indeed over here illegally, but do your best.

'Finally, Ian and Amanda – I want court orders raised today to seize Sutton Site Security records and computers for forensic examination immediately. In particular, we're looking for documentary evidence as to how they were removing the stolen equipment from John Brancourt's yard and any other extortion rackets that might have resulted in Damien's death.'

Sergeant Hughes raised his hand. 'Do you want me to organise a team to go to the premises when you have those, guv?'

'Please,' said Kay. She held up the report. 'Someone at Mark Sutton's business knows what's going on, and I'm betting if we squeeze hard enough, we'll find the answers. Let's get a move on.'

THIRTY-THREE

Six hours later, Kay followed Carys across to the table where Gary Hudson sat next to his solicitor.

He'd lost some of the swagger he'd had when she last saw him, a deep furrow appearing between his eyebrows as he saw the thick file Carys placed in front of Kay before opening her notebook and reaching across to the recording equipment.

Kay listened while her colleague read out the formal warning and then savoured the silence that followed.

Hudson fidgeted in his seat, then took a breath.

'Perhaps you could explain to my client why he's here?' said the solicitor. 'He's a busy man, DI Hunter, and his time is valuable. He's already spoken to you to help with your enquiries and has no other information to offer.'

Kay opened the file, and then slid across a photograph of Adrian Sutton. 'When did this man start working for Sutton Site Security?'

Hudson blinked. 'Barry? About two years ago.'

'What's his surname?'

'Esher.'

'Where's he from?'

'No idea.'

'Do you call him by any other name?'

'No.'

'Does Mark Sutton call him by any other name?'

Hudson shrugged. 'I don't think so.'

'Really?' Kay smiled at Hudson, and then pulled a photocopied certificate from the file and placed it on the table next to the photograph. 'See, we know Barry Esher was born Adrian Sutton. He's Mark's cousin, isn't he?'

Hudson's jaw worked, but he stayed silent.

'Did you know Barry Esher was related to Mark Sutton?' said Carys.

'He might have mentioned it.'

'He's got a hell of a reputation, hasn't he?'

'What do you mean?'

Carys flipped her notebook to a different page.

'Actual bodily harm, intimidation – is he really the sort of person you'd want working for a reputable security company?'

'That's not for me to say.'

'Whose idea was it to employ him?'

'Mark, I suppose. I don't know. He just turned up one day and Mark said he was able to help with a job we had on at the time.'

'Where was that?'

'Christ, I don't know – it was two years ago. You'd have to ask Mark. He'll probably have it written down somewhere.'

'We will,' said Kay. 'Who has the final decision on new employees?'

'Mark, of course. He's the boss.'

'Did Barry work on the Petersham Building project over the summer?'

'I don't think so, no. He was managing a job over in Thanet somewhere.'

Kay pushed a different document towards him. 'Then explain to me why he signed in at the Petersham Building on June twenty-seventh, the day Damien Brancourt went missing.'

Hudson leaned closer to run his eyes down the page, but kept his hands in his pockets. Finally, he looked up. 'I don't know.'

'But weren't you managing that site?'

'It doesn't mean I was there all the time. That's what we have staff for.' A smug smile twitched his features.

'So, you're telling me you never saw Adrian Sutton – Barry Esher – at the Petersham Building that day?'

'That's right.'

Kay's heart skipped a beat, but she kept her face passive as she pulled out a photograph from the folder and slapped it in front of him.

'Then perhaps you can explain why we have this CCTV image of you and Adrian next to the Queen Victoria monument on the High Street at three-thirty that afternoon.'

Hudson's Adam's apple bobbed as a panicked expression crossed his face.

His solicitor placed a hand on his arm.

'I'd like to take a moment with my client, please, Detective Hunter.'

'Thought you might.'

Kay swept the documents and photograph into the folder, ended the interview recording and followed Carys from the room.

'What do you think?' said Carys after she'd

closed the door and moved further along the corridor away from the interview room.

'He's going to try to distance himself from whatever the Suttons were up to,' said Kay. 'Hudson's already done time, and he's not going to want to go back to prison in a hurry.'

'Perhaps he knows they killed Damien.'

'Perhaps.' Kay turned as the solicitor appeared in the corridor and beckoned to her. 'Okay, let's find out.'

She waited until Carys restarted the recording and recited the date and time, and then folded her hands on the table. 'All right, Gary. What do you want to say to us?'

'Mark Sutton told me to meet Barry – Adrian – in Maidstone that afternoon. All I did was pass a mobile phone to him and tell him to expect a call from Mark later that day.'

'Was this mobile phone different to Adrian's usual phone?'

'Yeah.'

'Why would Mark do that?'

'I don't know. I swear, I don't know. I gave him the phone, then drove back to the office. That's it. That's all I did.'

'Did you see Adrian go in the Petersham Building?'

'No.'

'What direction did he go in when you parted ways?'

'I don't know. He made me go first. Said he didn't need me to hang about.'

'Did you look back?'

'No. I know when to follow orders.' He sat up straighter. 'Mark runs a tight ship, all right? He might have been a bit of a lad in his younger days, but he knows what he's doing. He has good people working for him.'

Kay drummed her fingertips on the desk, and frowned. 'Then why would Mark take on Adrian knowing he had a previous record for actual bodily harm?'

Hudson spread his hands. 'Everyone deserves a second chance, Detective Hunter.'

THIRTY-FOUR

The man who sat across the table from Kay and Carys in interview room four had the look and presence of someone who had done time and savoured the reputation.

Adrian Sutton had none of the looks or charm his cousin possessed. His nose had been broken in several places over the years, and he confirmed his name with a voice laced with hatred.

Kay lifted the cover of the file before her. 'Well, well you have been a busy man, haven't you?'

His jaw clenched. 'I haven't broken the law.'

'CCTV images from Maidstone High Street show you meeting Gary Hudson and taking a mobile phone from him,' said Kay and spun the photograph around to show him. 'Why?'

'It was broken and needed to be fixed.'

'Are you saying he couldn't arrange to do that himself?'

'I'm in charge of things like that.'

'So, why meet in the middle of Maidstone? Why would Mark tell him to do that?'

'Dunno. You'll have to ask Mark. He's the boss.'

'Did you threaten John Brancourt in order to get the work at the Petersham Building?' said Kay.

'What?'

'You heard me.'

'Don't be daft. That's illegal, and I told you – I haven't broken the law.'

'But you have in the past, haven't you? Before you worked for Sutton Site Security. What job is it you do for your cousin?'

Adrian sneered in response, but stayed silent.

Carys smiled and held up the deed poll. 'These are really only as good as the paper they're written on, Adrian. Your original name still appears on record. You might tell people to call you Barry Esher, but that's as far as it'll get you. It's not as if you can change your fingerprints as easily, is it? So, what does your role at Sutton Site Security entail?'

'Not much.'

'Really? Well, for someone who's not doing much

you're being well paid, aren't you?' Kay tugged a sheaf of bank statements from the folder and held them out. 'I'm guessing these don't show everything Mark's paying you. Just enough to make it all seem legitimate, right? Cash in hand for the rest?'

She shoved the security sign-in sheet across the table. 'Why did you go to the Petersham Building after meeting Gary Hudson?'

'Can't remember. It was a while back. Probably checking on progress.'

'Why?'

'Mark wanted to find out how the schedule was going. He had some bids lined up for new work.'

'Why couldn't he check himself? He went to the project meetings, didn't he?'

'Most of the time.'

'So, why send you?'

He eyed Kay with undisguised malice. 'He's a busy man, detective. What's the point in employing someone and then do the job yourself?'

'Who did you meet with?'

'A bunch of people – different contractors.'

'And what did you discuss?'

He blinked. 'I can't remember exactly. How things were going, if the project was going to finish on time – things like that.'

'Did you meet with John Brancourt while you were there?'

'Never saw the bloke.'

'What about his son, Damien?'

'Eh?'

'Damien Brancourt. Did you meet with him at the Petersham Building that day?'

'No.'

Kay held up a photograph taken at the crime scene by one of Harriet's team, and Adrian's solicitor recoiled, his eyes wide.

'Why did you kill Damien Brancourt?'

The solicitor recovered from his shock and slapped his hand on his notebook. 'Detective, that's—'

'I didn't kill Damien Brancourt,' said Adrian. 'I never saw him at the Petersham Building. The only time I ever saw him was when he tagged along with his father to hand over the keys to the place when we won the contract.'

'Won the contract? You threatened John Brancourt and removed equipment from his premises to blackmail him until he awarded the work to Sutton Site Security.'

'I don't know anything about that. You'd have to speak to Mark.'

'How did you steal John Brancourt's equipment from his yard?'

'I didn't.'

Kay turned to Carys. 'Show Mr Sutton the photographs we've obtained.'

The detective constable reached into a folder and pulled out a set of CCTV images Gavin had handed to her moments before they'd walked into the interview room. 'Cash withdrawals were made from various ATMs around the town the morning before each plant machine was stolen,' she said. 'And we have loading equipment on camera here at two forty-five in the morning on the road outside Brancourt's yard.'

'John Brancourt may be too frightened to report you and your cousin,' said Kay. 'But it doesn't stop us from investigating the theft.'

'Wasn't me.'

'But you know who was responsible, don't you?'

THIRTY-FIVE

Kay eyed Mark Sutton as Barnes read out the formal interview caution, noting that the man's heavyset eyes appeared bored rather than concerned at the turn of events.

Beside him, a slim well-dressed solicitor pressed pen to paper, his lips pursed as he jotted notes to himself.

Kay's gaze dropped to the business card the man had handed to her upon entering the interview room.

Andrew Faircroft.

Not a local, that was for sure. The telephone number embossed under his name displayed an outer London area.

She wondered fleetingly what a Kent security contractor was doing with a London-based legal representative, then refocused on the interview at hand and flipped open the folder before her as Barnes finished speaking.

'How many staff do you have working for you, Mr Sutton?' she said.

'I can't remember off the top of my head,' said Sutton, a sly smirk at the corner of his mouth.

'Try.'

He blew out his cheeks. 'Maybe thirty, forty people.'

'Full time? Part time?'

'A dozen full time. They act as managers for me on our different site contracts. The rest come and go as we need them.'

'And how do you pay those staff?'

He scowled. 'My business is all above board. I pay my taxes.'

Now it was Kay's turn to smile. 'You pay tax for the staff you actually put through your books, Mr Sutton. However, we've had someone look into your financial habits and it appears that your business is doing better than your taxable income provides for.' She snatched up two pages from the folder, placing them in front of Sutton and Faircroft. She tapped the left-hand one with her fingernail. 'These are surveillance reports from the past two Thursday mornings. Pay day for your casual staff, isn't it? Cash, too? I must say, there are a lot of men who turn up at your offices between the hours of seven and ten o'clock who leave with stuffed envelopes in their hands. How do you explain that?'

Sutton leaned his forearms on the table. 'Now, see here. Those are legitimate payments to casual workers.'

'They may well be,' said Kay, gesturing to the numbers displayed on the pages before him. 'But they don't appear in your tax returns, do they?'

She didn't wait for him to answer. Instead, she pulled another document from the folder and began leafing through it. 'Our forensic investigator provided this report to me this morning,' she said. 'It makes for an extremely interesting read. Even Barnes here was impressed, weren't you?'

'It's going to be a bestseller, I reckon,' said the detective sergeant. He took the report from Kay and held up the last page to Sutton. 'Money laundering, Mark. Not very clever in this day and age.'

The solicitor's eyebrows shot upwards. 'My client—'

'Has a lot of explaining to do,' said Kay. 'Now, why don't we start with the death of Damien Brancourt?'

'I had nothing to do with that!' Sutton pushed back his chair and pointed at Kay. 'You can't pin that on me.'

'Sit down,' Barnes barked.

The door swung open and two uniformed officers burst in, their faces alarmed.

Sutton sank into his chair and crossed his arms over his chest. 'Happy now?'

Kay nodded to the two officers. 'Thank you. We'll be fine.'

'If it's all the same to you, guv, I'll be outside the door in case you need me,' said the older constable.

Barnes waited until the door had closed, then turned back to Sutton. 'A lot of the men employed by you have criminal records, including your cousin Adrian. How would your clients feel knowing that you've forged security checks and passed these men off as legitimate security personnel?'

Sutton's jaw clenched.

'Did you use those men to steal the plant equipment from John Brancourt?' said Kay. 'We know you paid cash for the truck to take it away. Did you deliberately target John Brancourt because you wanted to get closer to Damien?'

'No. That's not what happened.'

'Then perhaps you could enlighten us?'

'Look,' said Sutton, and placed his arms on the table. 'I don't do the recruiting, all right? I leave that to Adrian. He knows people – the sort of people that can do the sort of work we need them to do. I don't ask questions.'

'You should,' said Kay. 'As their employer, the responsibility lies with you. And Adrian tells us you have the final say about everything to do with the business. You're the owner, after all. When did you instruct your men to steal the equipment?'

'It wasn't stolen. It was borrowed.'

Barnes laughed, and Kay fought to keep a straight face.

'Borrowed?' she said. 'Don't give me that. You stole it to coerce John Brancourt into awarding you the contract. You kept stealing equipment until he acquiesced.'

'No, he's mistaken. He must've forgotten. He told me we could borrow it for a few days, that's all.'

'Where's the loan agreement, then?'

Sutton's top lip curled. 'There was no paperwork. It was a gentlemen's agreement. Handshake. Probably slipped his mind with everything else he's had on this year.'

Kay looked up from her notes. 'What do you mean?'

'Ask him about the bailiffs. And the smaller contractors who've nearly gone out of business because he owes them money. I reckon he's got people chasing him for money on a daily basis. No wonder he's forgetting about loaning me equipment nine months ago. Reckon he's got bigger things to worry about at the moment.'

'How did Damien manage to get into the building if your men were meant to be guarding it?'

'I don't know.'

'Were you charging Brancourt for services you weren't delivering? Was there anyone actually guarding the building at night?'

He shrugged.

'What were your movements on June twenty-seventh?'

'I was stuck in the office. I was meant to be going to the site to do a check on progress, but I couldn't get away so I sent Adrian. I told him to keep his ears open. If John Brancourt was struggling to pay smaller contractors, I didn't want him trying to get out of paying me.'

'Otherwise there would be consequences?' said Kay. 'The sort of consequences that resulted in Damien Brancourt's death?'

'I didn't kill anyone. Never would,' said Sutton. 'Not good for business, see?'

'Speaking of which,' said Kay and closed her file, 'we'll be looking further into your business, Mr Sutton, I can assure you of that. You and I will be spending quite some time together.'

THIRTY-SIX

Kay threw the file onto her desk, failed to suppress a yawn and then signalled to Carys and Gavin to join her.

She pushed open the door to DCI Sharp's old office and ran her hand through her hair as her eyes fell on the darkened sky beyond the window. She turned as Gavin shut the door.

'Mark Sutton may be guilty of blackmail, theft and whatever Amanda Miller and her team can throw at him from a financial regulation point of view, but I think he's telling us the truth about Damien Brancourt. I don't think he's responsible for his death.'

'Are you sure, guv?' said Carys. 'I mean, he's got some pretty dodgy people working for him.'

'None of whom are in a hurry to go back to prison.'

'I've been going through the statements uniform have been collating from other construction companies who have used Sutton Site Securities,' said Gavin, 'and although none of them will admit to being blackmailed they do say that once his people are on site, there were no problems. In fact, the instances of theft from site went down dramatically.'

'Probably because of Sutton's reputation,' said Kay. 'Anyone who knew him and his men were probably too scared to nick anything.'

'So we let him go?' said Carys.

'For now. I think there's more to this than we're seeing at the moment,' said Kay. 'I want you to take a closer look at the other contractors that were working on site and who were engaged directly by John Brancourt. You can ignore anyone employed by Alexander Hill.'

She stopped talking at the sound of scratching at the door and pulled it open.

Barnes hurried inside, three pizza boxes balanced in one hand as he unbuttoned his coat with the other.

Kay took the boxes from him, handed over cash for the food and then gestured to her colleagues to help themselves while she paced the carpet.

'Eat this before it gets cold, guv,' said Gavin.

She sighed, then joined them and helped herself to a large slice of pepperoni-covered dough.

'Why the John Brancourt angle, guv?' said Carys. 'Why not Hill?'

'Sutton says Brancourt owed – and maybe still owes – a lot of people some money. Smaller contractors, tradespeople, that sort of thing. If one of those people was having problems getting money out of him and had tried the usual official channels, maybe they took matters into their own hands and used Damien as leverage.'

'Is it worth speaking to John Brancourt again?' said Barnes.

'We will, but not yet. Did you manage to trace Damien's last movements?'

'No sign of him on any CCTV imagery – the angles of the cameras on nearby buildings don't give us enough range,' said Gavin. 'We've got a picture of John Brancourt's car passing under a camera at the motor vehicle dealership on the A20 but that's after he dropped off Damien – there's no passenger in the car. None of the licensees or staff from the pubs in the Sittingbourne Road area that uniform spoke to recognised Damien's photo, either.'

'Well he and his friend must've gone somewhere

after John dropped him off,' said Kay. 'What about taxi firms?'

'We've contacted all the local cab companies, guv,' said Carys. 'Two drivers looked promising, but both of those checked out – one passenger was a businessman at Loose, and the other was a bloke over from the States who was visiting family in Allington. No sign of Damien.'

'Dammit,' said Kay. 'This is ridiculous. One of these people knows something.'

'Is it worth interviewing his brother and sister?' said Barnes. 'Maybe he said something to them about where he was really going?'

'We can try, but I want it done at their house. I'm not bringing two kids into the station – too traumatic for them given what's happened to their brother.'

'I'll make a note to speak to them over the weekend. I'll take Debbie with me – she's good with teenagers.'

'Okay, thanks.' She paused, and then wandered over to a spare whiteboard against the wall and picked up a pen. 'I think it's time we ran another media conference and use it to ask for the public's help in tracing Damien's movements.'

'Do you mean have a reconstruction?' said Carys.

'Exactly. Can you get onto the media team in the

morning? There'll be no time to organise anything tonight. I want everything we know about Damien's last day presented to the public – including dinner at his parents' house. We need the public to care about Damien. He was loved by his family, ran into a bit of trouble with us but worked his way through it and had a promising career ahead of him after getting his degree.' Kay wrote the filming scope on the board as she spoke. 'I want to show John driving Damien to Maidstone and leaving him at that bus stop.'

Gavin looked up from his notebook. 'How do we present the circumstances of his death?'

Kay re-capped the pen. 'Carefully. Don't sensationalise this, Gav. Might simply be a case of the presenter doing a piece to camera – or I can. Appeal to the public to come forward if they know anything that might help. I'll speak to headquarters in the morning about getting some bums on seats to answer phones once the media release goes out and the reconstruction is shown on television.'

She glanced up at a knock on the door, and then grinned at the familiar face that peered around it.

'You made it.'

'Wouldn't miss pizza for the world,' said Sharp.

He greeted the other detectives, helped himself to

a slice of pizza and then raised his glass of soft drink against theirs. 'Right, what's going on, then?'

Kay brought him up to speed in between mouthfuls of pizza. 'And today, we lost our prime suspect,' she finished.

'You don't think Mark Sutton is involved?'

'Not in the way we thought he was, no. I don't think he was responsible for Damien's death. He might have an inkling as to what's going on, but he's keeping quiet.'

'Protecting his own backside,' Barnes growled.

'Unfortunately, people like Mark Sutton will always look after themselves before anyone else.' Sharp's mouth twisted. 'It's why he and his ilk are so successful.'

'Ever had a run-in with him before, guv?' said Gavin.

'No – which shows how clever he's been to keep off our radar. No matter what happens with this investigation, I want us to pursue a separate enquiry into his business. It's obvious he's running a corrupt line in security, but we need something to charge him with.'

'Well, Amanda Miller has a lot of documentary evidence she's taking back to headquarters on Monday,' said Kay. 'That should make his life uncomfortable for a while, especially when she passes that on to Revenue and Customs.'

'It's a start,' said Sharp.

'Doesn't solve who was responsible for shoving Damien into that cavity, though,' said Barnes.

'Two steps forward, one step back,' said Carys.

'It's like the murder investigation version of bloody tango,' said Barnes. He snatched up a napkin and dabbed at his chin. 'So, what do we do next?'

'I'm hoping someone will come forward about Damien Brancourt's movements and what the hell he was doing coming back to Maidstone when everyone we've spoken to has assured us he was on his way to Heathrow to catch that flight to Nepal,' said Kay. 'And, hopefully, the televised reconstruction will help jog people's memory. Someone out there must know something.'

'What if they don't, guv?' said Carys, her voice barely above a whisper.

'I don't know,' said Kay. 'I really don't know.'

THIRTY-SEVEN

Kay glanced up from her computer screen as Barnes
dropped his backpack onto his chair the following
morning and ran his hand through sodden hair.

'Bloody rain. That'll teach me to leave home late
and end up having to park at the supermarket.'

She grinned and opened the bottom drawer of her
desk before tossing a clean towel to him. 'Use that.
I've been caught out before.'

'Cheers.'

He shrugged off his jacket, then dried his hair as
he walked around to where she sat. 'Anything
come in?'

'Nothing new to help us. Debbie's working with
Hughes and Parker to collate everything we know to
date about this case so we can do an audit over the

weekend. And we're going to lose four of the uniform team on Monday – Sharp's tried to argue the case with management, but there aren't enough people to go around because of the budget cuts.'

'Dammit. That's the last thing we need at the moment.'

'I know.' She sighed. 'Not a lot we can do about it, though.'

The door opened and Carys burst through, shoving a soaking wet umbrella into a plastic bag.

'I hope Damien Brancourt appreciates this,' she grumbled. 'If there was ever a time to have a duvet day…'

Kay laughed. 'Don't give me that. You wouldn't miss this for the world.'

A quirk began at the side of Carys's mouth. 'True. Where's Gavin?'

'Buying breakfast. I figured no-one would notice the difference with his hair if he got caught in the rain. He should be back soon. I presumed you'd both want bacon butties.'

Barnes's stomach rumbled loudly in response. 'You're a legend, guv.'

'I can't concentrate if I'm hungry so trust me, it wasn't a charitable decision.'

On cue, Gavin appeared, his arms laden with

paper bags that he proceeded to distribute amongst his colleagues before sitting down and sinking his teeth into one of the sandwiches.

They munched in silence for a moment, and Kay's mind wandered to the next steps in the investigation.

If Damien had met with someone prior to his flight to Nepal and found himself in danger, why hadn't he attempted to call his parents to let them know that something was wrong? None of his friends or acquaintances that had been formally interviewed had given any indication that Damien had tried to contact them, so who had he met with?

'Carys, can you and Gavin spend this morning going over the witness statements we took at the beginning of the week and contact everyone we spoke to? Ask them specifically if Damien mentioned whether he was planning to travel to Nepal with someone, would you?'

'Why would he not tell his parents who he was going with?'

'Perhaps it was a new girlfriend, or someone they wouldn't have approved of – something like that. See what you can find out. John Brancourt says there was no-one else at the bus stop when he dropped his son off, so maybe Damien met his friend somewhere else and then walked to a pub.'

'Will do.'

'Do you think we're going to find another body?' said Barnes, his eyes worried. 'Do you think whoever killed Damien killed his friend as well?'

'I hope not,' said Kay. 'I'm working on the basis that he or she might know how Damien got into that ceiling cavity. We have to consider the fact that whoever he met with is also responsible for covering up his death. Besides, Harriet's team found no evidence to suggest anyone else had been placed in the cavity.'

'Guv!'

She craned her neck to peer over her computer monitor in time to see Debbie rushing towards her. 'What's up?'

The police constable held out some pages she'd collated from the printer. 'Take a look at this, guv. I stumbled across it when I was going through some old newspaper reports about Hillavon Developments.'

Kay frowned and ran her eyes down the report. 'Bloody hell.'

'What is it?' said Gavin, perching on the end of Barnes's desk.

'Alexander Hill – Hillavon Developments – had a minor shareholding in another development company with interests in Bromley,' said Debbie. 'Three years ago, a worker was killed on site by falling masonry, and the firm was fined a significant amount of money for dodgy health and safety practices. What if Damien Brancourt's death was an accident, and Alexander Hill covered it up rather than risk getting sued again? I mean, Lucas said he was electrocuted, right?'

Kay pursed her lips as she finished reading the news article and handed it over to Barnes. 'I agree, it's worth investigating. Especially given the fact that Hill didn't return Gavin's calls for several days at the start of our enquiries. Maybe it was Hill who Damien met with.'

'Do you think he was avoiding us on purpose, then?' said Carys. 'Getting his story straight as it were?'

'Could be, and it could've been a mistake taking our focus off him these past few days. Barnes – can you find that list of attending personnel that Hughes put together from Sutton Site Security's records? We need to find out how many times Hill went to the site to check progress.'

'Hill would have had a key, too, given that he owns the place,' said Barnes, scribbling into his notebook. 'Debbie – can you contact John Brancourt and ask him for a copy of all the meeting minutes if we don't have those already? There might be a clue amongst those if there were safety concerns on site.'

Debbie headed back to her desk, and Kay turned as her desk phone rang.

'It's Andy Grey over at headquarters,' said a voice. 'I thought you might be in early.'

'I'm not the only one,' she said. 'The whole team's here. What are you up to?'

'We've been working on Damien Brancourt's mobile phone with one of your uniformed colleagues over here,' said the digital forensics expert. 'Call logs came through from his provider at last, and there's an old text message we recovered that you might be interested in. Turns out Damien had a meeting scheduled with Alexander Hill a week prior to his supposed flight to Nepal.'

Kay pushed back her chair. 'How did you find the message if Damien had deleted it?'

Grey chuckled. 'We have our ways. I'm going to email over what we've got and I'll copy it to Debbie so she can update HOLMES.'

'Is that the only message that mentions Hill?'

'Yes. I've double checked everything, and that's all I've come up with.'

'That's great, thanks.'

Kay ended the call and updated to her team.

'Alexander Hill is now a significant person of interest. I want all the information you can find on him by the end of today. Barnes – come with me. I'm going to find out what John Brancourt knows about his son's meeting with Hill.'

THIRTY-EIGHT

John Brancourt opened the door to Kay and Barnes, his expression wary.

'What do you want?'

'A word, please, Mr Brancourt.'

He stepped aside and gestured to the kitchen. 'Go through. Annabelle's having a lie down. She's still in shock.'

Kay let Barnes go on ahead and then placed her hand on Brancourt's arm. 'We have a family liaison officer who can be with you this afternoon if you need support.'

He shook his head. 'We'd prefer to keep our grief to ourselves, detective. Thank you, though.'

He brushed past her and followed Barnes,

indicating to them to take seats at the kitchen table while he leaned against the sink.

Kay waited until Barnes had retrieved his notebook from his jacket pocket and then turned her attention back to Brancourt.

'How are the twins holding up?'

'All right, I suppose.' He shrugged. 'They're teenagers – they don't talk much at the best of times, so it's hard to tell.'

'What's your relationship with Alexander Hill like?'

'Relationship? I bid to work on some of his projects, and that's about it. Why?'

'How many projects of his have you bid on?'

'Probably a dozen over the years.'

'And how many did you win? How many have you worked on?'

'Three. The one at the Petersham Building, a housing project over near Aylesford and another office development at West Malling.'

'Ever socialise with him outside of work?'

'No. Not my type of person to be honest.'

'Oh? In what way?'

'A bit too cutthroat for my liking.' Brancourt pushed himself away from the sink. 'I run a business that's been in my family for three generations. We take care of our workers, pay our taxes and support local charities and businesses. Alex is – how can I put it – ruthless. It's all about the money to him.'

Kay let her gaze wander over the state-of-the-art appliances and shiny surfaces in the kitchen, then turned back to Brancourt. 'You appear to be doing all right, though by the looks of things.'

'We are, yes.'

'How's the business cash flow these days?'

'Pardon?'

'We've spoken to witnesses who have indicated that some of your contractors might not be getting paid on time.'

John snorted. 'Rumours, that's all. Believe me, detective. I look after my suppliers. I wouldn't have a business without them.'

'But you've struggled in the past?'

'Like everyone else did during the recession, yes. But I cut my overheads, saved wherever I could, and made sure everyone got paid.'

'Why would your son have a meeting scheduled with Alexander Hill a week before he disappeared?'

'What?'

'Our digital forensic team were able to retrieve a deleted message from Damien's mobile phone. A week before he died, he arranged to meet with Hill. Do you know what they discussed?'

'I-I haven't got a clue.' John moved to the table and sank into the seat next to Barnes. 'Why would he do that and not tell me?'

'That's what we're trying to establish before we speak to Mr Hill,' said Kay. 'Do you have any idea at all why your son was going to meet with him?'

'No. He never mentioned it.'

'Would he have spoken to your wife about it?'

'If he did, she would've told me.' Brancourt twisted the wedding band on his finger. 'We have no secrets in this household, detective.'

'And yet you didn't know about this meeting between your son and Alexander Hill.'

Brancourt sighed. 'Damien could be a bit too private for his own good sometimes. Have you found the friend he said he was meeting?

'We're working on it,' said Kay. 'Our colleagues have been interviewing licensees of pubs in the area as well as checking additional CCTV footage—'

She broke off as Annabelle Brancourt entered the kitchen, a chunky woollen cardigan draped over her shoulders and her hair pinned up.

The woman's face bore the lines of grief; her eyes

dull. 'What are you doing here? Have you found who killed my son?'

Kay's heart went out to the woman, but she kept her features passive. 'Not yet, Mrs Brancourt. My team and I are working around the clock to find the answers you need, though.'

Annabelle sniffed, then shuffled over to the worktop and flipped the switch on the kettle. 'I decided to keep Bethany and Christopher from going back to school at the end of last week. It's nearly the end of term anyway, and I couldn't bear the thought of them having to listen to all the gossip that must be going around while they're trying to study for their mock exams. Kids can be awful to each other.'

'They can,' said Barnes, pushing his chair back and walking over to the kettle that was now rumbling on its stand, a steady cloud of steam rising from its spout. He flipped the switch, then turned to Annabelle. 'I've got a daughter, out of her teens now, but she was a terror at school. Where'd you keep the cups?'

'Left-hand side of that cabinet there.'

'Sit yourself down. I'll make it.'

Kay caught her colleague's eye as she joined the Brancourts, and nodded a silent thanks before delving into her handbag for her notebook.

'Where are they now?' she said.

'Upstairs, in their bedrooms. Playing computer games, I expect,' said Annabelle. She brushed a wayward strand of hair from her forehead. 'Why?'

'I'd like to speak with them, if you don't mind, to see if Damien mentioned anything to them about this friend of his, or what his plans were for his trip to Nepal.'

'They weren't very close to him. There's an eight-year age difference between them and Damien.'

'Still…'

'I'd rather you didn't. Not yet. Give them a few more days to grieve in peace, please.' Annabelle glanced up as Barnes placed a cup of tea in front of her, and murmured her thanks. She wiped at her eyes, then lifted the cup and blew across the hot surface before staring at the liquid as if wondering what to do next with it.

Kay reached into her bag and pulled out a file before removing a page and sliding it across the table to John. 'We've found evidence to support your claim that Mark Sutton hired vehicles to remove the two generators from your yard last year,' she said.

Brancourt leaned forward and reached out with a shaking hand to pull the document closer. 'What is this?'

'All we need is your statement to the effect that Sutton was blackmailing you, and we can begin a separate investigation into the theft.'

He blinked, then pushed the page towards her. 'I don't think so, Detective Hunter. After all, no harm came of it. The equipment was returned in good condition.'

'Did Mark Sutton threaten you in the past?'

'What makes you say that?'

'When Damien was arrested at the protest, a witness stated that he told the man he assaulted to leave you alone. What was that about?'

'I can't remember.'

'John, Mark Sutton blackmailed you so you'd award him the work. You can't let him get away with that.'

The man's shoulders lifted, and then sagged once more. 'It's probably for the best if I don't. Can you see yourselves out? I really should be getting on. I've lots of paperwork to do, and phone calls to make.'

Kay fought down the frustration bubbling inside her, but gathered up her things before signalling to Barnes. 'If either Christopher or Bethany mention something about Damien's trip or any plans to meet someone in Maidstone prior to flying out, please – contact me immediately. My personal mobile number is on the card I gave to you. It doesn't matter what time of day or night it is. They might remember something important that will help us.'

Annabelle rose from her chair and gestured to the door. 'I'll see you out.'

Kay noticed that John didn't move as they followed her, and as she checked over her shoulder she saw that the man was now facing the window next to the kitchen table, his gaze unfocussed as he stared blankly through the glass.

Barnes paused at the front door, his hand on the doorknob. 'Mrs Brancourt, do you recall whether Damien was applying for any jobs at the time of his disappearance, or what his future plans were once he returned from Nepal?'

The woman frowned. 'Why would he apply for jobs? He was taking over the family business from John in a couple of years. We spoke before he went away – next year he was going to start a part-time Master of Business Administration and go and work for John to get to know the ropes a bit better. You know – ease him into managing the staff so it didn't come as a shock to them when he eventually took over.' A sad smile crossed her face. 'John was looking forward to a retirement where he could watch him expand the business and build it up from what he's managed to achieve. He was certainly capable.'

'All right, Mrs Brancourt, we'll be on our way. Like I said – if they say anything, anything at all that might help our investigation, please call me,' said Kay.

As the front door closed on her and she made her way back to the car with Barnes, a heavy weight settled in her chest.

'Grief is a bitch,' said Barnes.

She clipped her seatbelt into place, and raised her eyes to see two faces at an upstairs window, their expressions gaunt.

'It is, Ian. It certainly is.'

THIRTY-NINE

Alexander Hill glared over his wire-framed glasses at Kay.

'I don't appreciate being interrupted from a social gathering on a Sunday lunchtime by two of your uniformed officers and frogmarched to their car, detective.'

'Too bad,' she said, and flipped open the folder in front of her. She took a moment to collect her thoughts, ignoring the penetrating stare from Hill's solicitor.

She'd met the man before – a stalwart amongst the Kentish legal establishment, and one who held the unenviable reputation of being both the most expensive, as well as the most repugnant.

Finally, Kay snatched a page from the folder and

thrust it at Hill.

'This is a call log from Damien Brancourt's mobile phone. Specifically, a text message that you sent to him a week before his death.'

Hill's eyebrows shot upwards before he had a chance to recover. 'He told me he'd deleted it.'

'He had. Our digital forensics team are very good at what they do, though. Why did you arrange to meet with him?'

Hill cast a sideways glance at his solicitor, then shuffled in his seat.

'Okay,' he said. 'Look – all I wanted to do was speak to him about an opportunity I had for him. I didn't want John finding out.'

'What sort of opportunity?'

'One that couldn't be discussed over the phone.'

Kay glared at him. 'I haven't got the time or inclination to play games here, Mr Hill. Spit it out. What did you discuss with Damien Brancourt the week prior to his death?'

He shrugged. 'He's a smart person. I had a role come up that I thought would suit him.'

'What sort of role?'

'Business development. Damien was a very gifted person, Detective Hunter. He could've gone far in any career he chose.'

'We were under the impression he was going to take over the Brancourt family business within a few years.'

Hill snorted. 'He'd have been wasted there. It's why we didn't tell John about our meeting. He'd have started getting defensive about how the business was meant to stay in the family. Damien understood there's no room for sentiment in this day and age. He saw the future, and he saw it with Hillavon Developments.'

'Why did you avoid calls from my team after Damien's body was found?'

'I couldn't help it – I was busy.'

'You were playing golf.'

A faint blush appeared on Hill's cheeks and he lowered his gaze to his hands. 'It was a business meeting.'

'It gave you time to create an alibi for your movements around the time of Damien's disappearance, too.'

'I had nothing to do with that!'

Kay slipped a stapled sheaf of papers from the folder, flipped to the fourth page and then turned it around to face Hill, before stabbing her forefinger halfway down.

'This is the site security records kept by Sutton

Site Security. You went to the Petersham Building two days before Damien Brancourt disappeared. Why did you go there?'

'I had to go – we had a site meeting.'

'There are no other records to support that statement, Mr Hill. Every site meeting was minuted, wasn't it?'

His face fell. 'Yes.'

'So, it was an unscheduled visit?'

'Yes.'

'Why?'

'Look, I had some concerns about the work, that's all. I wanted to take a look for myself. It's all very well having scheduled site meetings to discuss the progress of a project, but sometimes the contractors discuss the issues when I'm not in attendance and come up with a way to disguise what's really going on – I didn't want to find out about something by accident. We were working to a very tight schedule.'

'Did you encourage your contractors to hurry their work in order to meet that schedule?'

'If you're implying my client cut corners from a health and safety perspective, detective—'

Kay glared at the solicitor. 'Strange that you should mention that, given your client's past record in that regard.'

Hill held up his hand before the solicitor could utter a retort. 'Hang on. There were no health and safety issues regarding the Petersham Building as far as I was aware. You've obviously heard about the project I was involved with three years ago – that was caused by ineffective training of an apprentice by a contractor of mine, and I paid a heavy fine for that. It was tragic.'

'For the apprentice, or your wallet?' said Barnes.

'What were your concerns related to on site at the Petersham Building?' said Kay. 'Why did you go there unannounced?'

'I'd heard a rumour that equipment was going missing,' said Hill. 'And then about a month after that, a consignment of fibre optic cabling for the communications wiring that was being installed disappeared.'

'What was the value of that?'

'Thousands,' said Hill. 'And no-one could tell me where it was, or what had happened to it.'

'What did Mark Sutton have to say about it? Weren't his people providing security for the building?'

'Whoever took the cabling did it over the space of a Friday and Saturday night – Sutton's already told me he only had one man in attendance that weekend because of a rock music event he was contracted for. Apparently, they paid him more than I did so my project didn't warrant the protection it deserved.'

'When did you find out about the theft?'

Hill jabbed his finger at the site security attendance sheet. 'That morning when I turned up. I wondered why everyone was avoiding me. It was only when I demanded to know what was going on that I found out. After that, the proverbial hit the fan – I ended up in the middle of a shouting match between John Brancourt and Mark Sutton two days later when I had them come over to my office that afternoon to explain themselves.'

'Did you find out who took it?' said Barnes.

'No.'

'Why wasn't the theft reported to the police?' said Kay. 'We've got no record of any thefts from that site.'

'John said he'd deal with it. A day later, he managed to source some replacement cabling at short notice. He cracked the whip on site and managed to pull the schedule back on track.'

'Did Damien accept the job you offered to him?'

'What?'

'The business development role you said you discussed with Damien. Did he take it?'

'He said he was going to come back to me and let me know. I never heard from him again.' Hill twisted one of his cuff links, and blinked. 'And that's something I'll always regret.'

'The game of golf you said you were playing – sorry, the business meeting – you left early. Why was that?'

'I didn't—'

'Be careful what you say, Mr Hill. We have witness statements from two of your associates claiming that you only played nine holes, not eighteen. Why did you leave early?'

Hill quickly glanced at his solicitor, then back. 'I met with Mr Caplan here, at his office. W-when I heard about Damien's death, I panicked, that's all.'

'Interesting.' Kay pulled the documentation across the table and closed the folder before pushing her chair back. 'With me, Barnes.'

She moved towards the door, then paused as Hill called out.

'Detective Hunter?'

Kay glanced over her shoulder to see Hill on his feet, his face distraught. 'What?'

'I didn't kill Damien Brancourt. You have to believe me. He was like a son to me.'

FORTY

Kay slumped in her seat and glared at the highlighted emails on her computer screen, counting the number of messages that had appeared since she'd been speaking to Alexander Hill and wondering how many of them she could delegate amongst her colleagues.

'How did it go, guv?' said Carys. She pulled a chair over and crossed her legs, her pen poised over her notebook.

'I'm not sure.' Kay held down three keys to lock the computer screen, then turned to her. 'I think he was shocked that we found the message – he and Damien were definitely hiding the fact that they'd met, and they didn't want John Brancourt finding out.'

'Because John wanted Damien to take over his business.'

'Exactly, and it seems Hill was closer to Damien than John might have been, especially–'

She broke off as DCI Sharp entered the room and hurried towards her.

'Guv?'

'Sorry, Kay – I've just heard from the Superintendent. We don't have enough evidence against Alexander Hill to hold him any longer. We have to let him go if we're not going to charge him.'

'But he's only been here six hours,' said Barnes. 'We don't need a magistrate's approval yet.'

'It's political,' said Sharp. 'Hill has connections, and he's taking advantage of that.'

'Dammit.' Kay turned and slapped her hand against the side of the filing cabinet.

'Have you got anything to suggest he was directly involved with Damien's death?'

'No, guv.'

'Then I'm sorry, Kay. We'll make sure he hands in his passport just in case, but we have to release him.' Sharp turned to Gavin. 'Piper, could you go and organise that when we've finished here?'

'Guv.'

Sharp moved across to the whiteboard and crossed

his arms as he worked his way through the notes Kay had added over the course of the investigation. Finally, he gave a slight nod.

'I know it's frustrating, Hunter. But, keep digging. Someone on that site is lying. We simply haven't found out who yet.'

'Guv.'

'I'll be over at headquarters first thing tomorrow. Keep me posted on any developments.'

He gave a curt nod, murmured his thanks to the team, and left.

Kay turned back to the uniformed team, their faces drawn under the pale yellow light from the ageing fluorescent fittings. 'All right, you lot. That's enough for the day. See you at eight o'clock tomorrow. Piper – you'd better head downstairs and get the paperwork started to release Hill and sort out that passport being handed in.'

She waited until they had started to file out of the door, then leaned forward and wiggled her mouse until her computer screen illuminated and brought up the files for the case, running her gaze over each entry before discarding it, frustrated she couldn't find what she sought. She glanced up as Barnes leaned against her desk and smiled.

'What?'

'I know that look, guv,' he said. 'What are you doing?'

'Can't keep anything from you, can I?'

'No, so spit it out.'

'Have you got the phone number for Marcus Weston, the operations manager at the software company?'

Barnes flipped through his notebook. 'Yes. Here you go.'

Kay stabbed the number into her desk phone, and then exhaled in frustration as she listened to the voicemail message. 'He's in Canada until next week.'

'What were you going to ask him?'

'I wanted to take another look at the cavity where Damien was found. Have we still got a key to the Petersham Building or was it returned to Weston after Harriet's lot finished with the crime scene?'

'I think Debbie had one she was going to take over there sometime and let them know they can use the room now that the CSIs have finished. I don't know if she's had a chance to yet, though.'

'Do you know where she put it?'

Kay rose from her chair and crossed the room to the police constable's desk.

The administrative detritus associated with a major investigation in full swing covered much of

Debbie's work area, despite her best attempts to keep the files and paperwork in separate piles for ease of reference.

'What are you thinking?' said Barnes as he joined her.

'The cavity Damien's body dropped out of – why put him in there in the first place? It was dark, there wasn't any CCTV facing the rear of the building, so why not carry him out of there and hide his body somewhere else? I want to take another look now, before that room gets handed back.'

'Okay, I've got an idea.' He waved his hand at the paperwork. 'Easier than going through this lot to try and find a key, anyway.'

'Oh yeah, what's that?'

He grinned. 'Gemma Tyson.'

'The receptionist?'

'I heard her talking at the scene the day Damien's body was discovered. She's a smart kid – and she has the security codes to the building, which you'll need as well as a key. She's renting a flat in Wheeler Street so she's just around the corner, too.'

Kay sucked in a breath. 'We'd need Gavin to stall Alexander Hill in case he was thinking about heading over there tonight. I know he wouldn't get into the building but I don't want him to see us if he drives past.'

'On it,' called Carys and picked up her phone.

'How long do you think we can delay him for?' said Barnes.

'An hour, no longer,' said Kay. 'His solicitor's experienced at this sort of thing. As long as Gav hasn't spoken to them yet—'

'He hasn't.' Carys put down her phone. 'He got waylaid by Hughes at the front desk to deal with a reporter, so I've told him to wait another twenty minutes before giving the good news to Hill and his solicitor. He reckons it'll take him a good forty to fifty minutes to do the paperwork after that because he's just hurt his hand and his writing will be slow.'

Kay smiled at the cheeky grin the detective constable wore, then checked her phone. 'Get onto Gemma, Barnes. Have her meet us outside the Petersham Building in fifteen minutes.'

FORTY-ONE

A quarter of an hour later, Kay waited until a taxi pulled away from the kerb with its inebriated occupants and then nodded to Gemma Tyson.

'Now.'

Few pedestrians remained on the High Street, a cold wind and horizontal rain keeping most people indoors.

Kay caught Barnes's eye and he winked as a quiet *beep* reached their ears.

'Here we go, guv.'

Gemma held open one of the double doors for Kay and Barnes to enter, then locked it behind them. 'You'll need to wait there while I turn off the alarm for the rest of the building.'

She disappeared behind the reception desk,

switched on a desk lamp beside her computer and keyed in a sequence of numbers before straightening. 'Okay, follow me.'

'Not so fast,' said Kay. 'We'll take it from here.'

The receptionist's face fell.

'Here's my mobile number,' said Barnes. 'Can you call me if anyone else shows up?'

'Will do.'

He led the way through to the main office interior, switched on the lights and then headed across the large space and up a staircase, his shoes echoing off the metal treads in the silence of the building.

Kay followed, her excitement at the prospect of what they might discover tempered by the anxiety that it could be a fruitless task.

She was running out of options.

Barnes reached the top of the stairs and pushed the door open into the office above the breakout area. He gestured to Kay to step inside.

'At least we don't have to try to remove the carpet and underlay – it hasn't been put back yet.'

'Good. I didn't fancy trying to pull that up. Let's have a look, shall we?'

She retrieved a photograph taken by Harriet's team when they had been called to the scene from her pocket, and paced back and forth across the bare floor, scrutinising the markings that had been highlighted by the crime scene investigators.

'There are drag marks here, look. You can see where the boards have been scuffed.'

'But they go towards the cavity, not towards the door.'

'So moving him outside was never an option.' Kay frowned. 'That means the cavity was open before Damien died. Why?'

She dropped to the floor beside the loose boards that remained from the CSIs' intrusion, then gestured to Barnes to help her. 'We need to look inside here.'

Pulling a thin torch from her jacket pocket as Barnes pushed the first of the floorboards away, she shone the beam into the gap. 'Can you move another one?'

Kay lowered her face until her cheek rested on the floor, and swung the beam around to her left. She shifted until she could see better into the cavity, and then straightened and sat back on her heels.

'Well, that's interesting.'

'What is it?' said Barnes.

In reply, Kay pulled out her mobile phone and hit the speed dial. 'Gavin? Is Alexander Hill still at the station? Get down to the car park and bring him back in, now. He's got some explaining to do.'

KAY HANDED her rain-soaked jacket to the uniformed officer outside the interview room, then pushed open the door and approached the table where Alexander Hill sat with his solicitor.

'What is the meaning of this?' said the solicitor. 'I demand an explanation.'

'One moment,' said Kay, then indicated to Barnes to read out the formal caution once the recording equipment was running. That done, she turned back to Hill.

'What do you know about the contractors responsible for the wiring in the Petersham Building?'

'Only that John Brancourt brought in a team from Brighton to do it – they weren't cheap, but they were thorough. They won the contracts for the fibre optic cabling for the software company's computer servers as well as all the telecommunications equipment. Why?'

'Tell me about the copper wiring in the ceiling cavity. We took a look and none of the old wiring has been removed. All the new wiring is over the top of it.'

'What about it?'

'What's it doing there? We have whole teams

working with the British Transport Police over metal theft because of the value of copper. That stuff's being stolen from the side of railways and old telephone exchanges up and down the country. If you were renovating a building, why didn't you remove the copper wiring and sell it on?'

Hill clasped his hands together on the table. 'We were going to, but like I told you before, we were behind on the schedule. If I'd insisted on paying the electrical contractor to remove the copper wiring before installing the new fibre optic cables and other wiring, it would have added another four weeks to the project, never mind the cost involved. I simply couldn't afford for the completion date to be pushed back. It made more sense to leave the copper wiring in place.' He shrugged. 'The software company has a tenancy for ten years. I can always arrange for someone to come back and remove the copper wiring at the end of their lease if I decide to sell it before a new tenant goes in.'

Kay removed her mobile phone and selected the photos app before passing it across to Hill. 'That's what I thought. But I've just taken a look at that cavity where Damien Brancourt's body was found, and saw this.'

Hill frowned, but took the phone from her and

looked at the screen. A split second later, his mouth dropped open. 'That doesn't make sense. '

'That's what I thought,' said Kay. 'The copper wiring has been cut. And it looks like it's been pulled out of place – not left in situ as you've just described. Now, I know that Damian's bodyweight would have moved the wiring as it worked its way through the cavity over time, but not like that.'

Hill passed her phone back. 'None of the contractors would have touched that. We made it very clear at the project meeting in early June that that copper wiring was staying in place. Anyway, none of them would have cut it – it was still live. It's powering the old telephone lines the bank had installed. If anyone tried to cut those, they'd be—'

'Electrocuted,' said Kay. 'Exactly. Damian Brancourt was stealing the copper wire from the Petersham Building when he was killed.'

FORTY-TWO

'Come on, grab a seat. Let's get a move on.'

Kay called across the room to the assembled investigation team the next morning, the sound of the last chair scraping across the carpet reaching her as she turned to the whiteboard and gestured to the photograph of Damien Brancourt.

'For those of you who have just arrived, we're now certain Damien was electrocuted while trying to steal copper wire from the Petersham Building. Alexander Hill neglected to inform us when we first spoke with him that the copper wire was still live at the time of the renovations and was left in place for future retrieval. Damien Brancourt obviously had other ideas.'

'When do you want to tell his parents?' said Barnes.

'Not yet. I want more answers before we give them the news, especially given Alexander Hill's statement that Damien wasn't interested in working for the family business. I want to find out from Damien's friends why he felt that way. And the copper theft – what motivated Damien and his accomplice? Why did they need the money?'

She gestured to Debbie to begin handing out copies of the day's report extracted from HOLMES. 'Hughes, Parker – I want you working with Gavin to find out who buys salvaged copper around this area. If none of the companies you speak to have dealt with Damien, then widen your search. Trading Standards will have a list of metal recyclers, so start with those. Have a word with our colleagues in burglary as well. Remember, copper theft is a major source of income for organised crime members. We tread carefully with this information, and with the people we're going to be questioning. I want to know if Damien Brancourt and his accomplice were planning to deal with one salvage company or several to spread the risk of getting caught.'

Barnes held up his hand. 'There are trade associations that deal with metal salvage, too guv. I'll make some phone calls and find out if there have been any complaints made about their members.'

'Thanks, Ian.' Kay took a step back from the board so she could review her case notes. 'We've missed something along the way. Stealing copper from a building with a private security company in attendance takes guts – not to mention a healthy amount of stupidity.'

'Could he have been coerced into the metal theft, guv?' said Carys.

'I certainly want to speak to Mark Sutton again before we rule that out,' said Kay. 'Can you bring him in for questioning this morning?'

'Should we re-interview his university acquaintances?' said Gavin. 'Maybe they were working on the theory that they could sell it to pay off any university debt quickly.'

'That's a fair point, and one worth considering. I want to speak to Julie Rowe. She seems to have a knack for coming up with the ideas but coercing others into carrying out her actions. Case in point – Damien getting into trouble at that protest while she simply stood by. She didn't mind taking the credit in the local newspapers for the protest, but she let Damien take the fall for her when things turned nasty.'

'She's going to make a great politician,' said Barnes.

'Indeed.' Kay craned her neck to see over the assembled team. 'Is Amanda here?'

'Yes, guv.' The financial investigator wound her way between the desks towards her.

'Can you conduct a review on ELMER for Damien Brancourt, Julie Rowe, Shaun Browning and the others to see what state their financial affairs are in? Credit card debts, overdraft facilities, the lot. I want to know if any of them have been struggling to pay off debt, or conversely have large cash deposits being made in the twelve months leading up to Damien's death.'

'Will do. It'll take me the rest of the day to put that together, but I can have it on your desk before I leave today.'

'Thank you. Best make a start while we finish here.' Kay picked up her briefing notes. 'Hughes – I want you to work with the local branch of the British Transport Police. I'm particularly interested to hear about anyone caught stealing metal of any kind in the past year, or suspected of doing so. Find out if they've got any contacts we can speak to confidentially about Damien Brancourt – someone out there must know something. Even if it was the first time Damien had participated in metal theft, the person he was with was evidently cool-headed enough to remove the copper wire that had been cut in order to sell it. That indicates to me that person has had practice.'

'Yes, guv.'

'Back to Mark Sutton – I want an immediate audit of the financial records we have for him to find out if there are any links between his security work and salvage yards. When you're talking with local companies, ask who they buy from – including cash purchases. Be cautious when you do so, because I don't want to warn off Sutton before we've had a chance to fully investigate this angle.'

'Noted, guv,' said Gavin.

'Right, that's it – dismissed. Barnes – get onto Julie Rowe, and let me know when she's here.'

FORTY-THREE

Kay buttoned her jacket and then gave the door to interview room four a hard shove.

The gesture had the desired effect, with both Julie Rowe and her solicitor jumping in their seats at the noise.

The solicitor recovered faster, turning the page of his notebook and straightening his tie with an audible huff as Kay sat opposite his client.

Julie Rowe appeared paler than Kay remembered from their last meeting and as Barnes recited the formal caution, she wondered how much the twenty-something was regretting her dalliance with Damien Brancourt.

'My client has already provided a full statement about her interaction with Mr Brancourt,' said the solicitor. 'She feels this latest intrusion on her life is unnecessary.'

Kay ignored him, and kept her gaze on Julie. 'How much credit card debt do you have?'

'I-I don't know off the top of my head.' Julie's eyes widened in panic as she glanced at her solicitor, then back. 'A few thousand pounds, maybe.'

'Let me refresh your memory,' said Kay, and took the folder Barnes held out. 'As at the thirtieth of last month, the balance owing is twelve thousand, six hundred and forty-two pounds. Plus interest at thirteen per cent.'

Barnes whistled through his teeth. 'How much of that was Christmas shopping?'

Julie jutted out her chin. 'None of your business. I'll have you know I work hard for a living. Bloody hard. If you're trying to make a point, Detective Hunter, then I'd appreciate hearing it.'

'How long do you expect to take to pay off this debt?' said Kay. 'Four years? Six? You're not working full-time at the moment, are you?'

'I really don't understand what my client's financial affairs have to do with your investigation, detective—'

'Then be quiet and listen,' Kay snapped. She glared at Julie. 'Damien Brancourt died because he was stealing copper wire from the Petersham Building. He and his accomplice didn't know that the wiring was still live, so when Damien cut it, he was electrocuted.'

She waited while Barnes pushed a photograph taken of Damien's body in situ on the breakout area floor across the table to Julie.

The young woman's eyes widened in shock, and then she brought a shaking hand to her mouth as she cried out.

'I'm running out of patience,' said Kay. 'I've spoken to every single person Damien came into contact with in the days and weeks leading up to his disappearance. One of you is lying.'

Julie shook her head, her eyes wet. 'It's not me. I've told you the truth.'

'But have you told me everything?' Kay retrieved the photograph and covered it with her hand. 'Julie, I think Damien Brancourt frightened you. You thought you could use him to get attention for your cause with the protests against the development works in town, didn't you, but you couldn't control his temper.'

'He didn't mean it.'

Julie's solicitor reached across to pluck a paper tissue from the box next to the recording equipment and passed it across to his client, his jaw set firm.

'Mean what?' said Kay once the woman had regained a little of her composure.

Julie dabbed at her eyes, then lowered shaking hands to her lap. 'He hit me.'

'When?'

'A few days after the protest. After the police dropped the charges.'

'What happened, Julie?' Kay softened her voice, keen to win the woman's trust. 'Why did Damien hit you?'

'He said it was my fault that he'd lashed out at that man. He said I used him.' She shrugged. 'I suppose he was right, I did.'

'That didn't give him an excuse to hit you.'

'It was just how he was. One minute you could be having a normal conversation with him, the next he'd be yelling in your face.'

'Was he always like that?'

'No, he wasn't. When I first met him at university he was a lot of fun. He was always the one who made the rest of us laugh.'

'Any idea why he changed?'

'I think he was under a lot of pressure. He owed money and I don't think his dad's business was doing that well and it was the stress of it all. He didn't know what to do. He didn't know how to cope.'

KAY FLICKED through the report on her desk, her chin in her hand as she ran her finger down the still-warm pages that had been printed out and shoved under her nose by Amanda Miller five minutes after she had finished interviewing Julie Rowe.

The noise in the incident room had dulled to a steady hum, a gradual emptying of the space as her colleagues had ended their shifts for the day, exhausted by frustration and an overwhelming sense of hopelessness as the case dragged on into its third week without a significant lead.

'How did you know, guv?' said Barnes. 'About Damien's temper, I mean.'

Kay sighed. 'I didn't, it was only a hunch. But the way Julie said he lashed out at Mark Sutton's security guard made me wonder if Damien had a problem controlling his anger. It seemed out of character compared with what we've heard about him from both his parents and Alexander Hill.'

'At least now we've got a better idea of his finances thanks to Julie. I wonder how he managed to keep that from his father – not to mention from his bank records? None of that came up in Amanda's search.'

'In all fairness, Amanda's only had a few hours to do some digging around. At least we know why Damien was angling for work with Alexander Hill though – he needed to get out of debt, and working for his father's company wasn't going to pay him enough.'

'What do you want to do next?'

'I want—'

'Guv!'

Kay broke off at Carys's shout from the other end of the incident room, and glanced over her shoulder to see the detective constable hurrying over to her.

'What is it?'

'Look at this – it's from ten years ago.'

She thrust a printout of a charge sheet at Kay and stood with her arms crossed while she read it.

'And that's not all, guv. Take a look at this.'

Kay's heart picked up its pace as she scanned the information. 'John Brancourt was arrested at a pub in Sutton Valence for punching one of the regulars,' she said, and then raised her gaze to Carys. 'Seems like Damien's father has a problem controlling his temper as well.'

An idea began to form as she watched Barnes read the new information, and she held up a finger to stop him interrupting her thoughts.

'Hang on. We've been looking at this the wrong way, haven't we? What if it wasn't Damien who was stealing the copper wire to pay off his debts?'

Barnes dropped the page to his lap as his jaw dropped open. 'Are you serious?'

'I am. With me, Ian – we're paying John Brancourt another visit. Now.'

FORTY-FOUR

Kay didn't wait for Barnes to pull the key from the ignition when he parked their pool car outside the front door of the Brancourts' property.

Instead, she unclipped her seatbelt and tore from the vehicle, hammering on the front door as her colleague joined her, out of breath.

'Bloody hell, guv. It's not like he's a flight risk – slow down.'

She ground her teeth, cursing aloud as the doorbell went unanswered, and then peered through the letterbox.

No-one moved inside; she could see the staircase newel post on the right and the fireplace that still smouldered, but there was no sign of John or Annabelle Brancourt – or their two teenagers.

'Guv?'

'Round the back. Maybe they're in the garden.'

Barnes glanced up at the overcast sky, his expression giving her no doubt as to his thoughts about the chances of finding the Brancourts outside in the middle of winter, but he led the way to the right and through an archway that had been cut into a stone wall.

Beyond the arch, an aroma of wood smoke wafted on the air and Kay fought down the sense of nausea that clenched at her stomach. Following a gruesome investigation the previous summer she hadn't been able to stand the smell and she cast her gaze around the sprawling grounds in an attempt to find a new focus.

A scraping sound reached her ears, and as she turned the corner of the house in Barnes's wake, she spotted Annabelle using a rake to gather twigs strewn around the trunk of a large horse chestnut tree that had been pruned.

The woman wore a woollen hat, her gloved hands protecting her from the worst of the elements and as Kay tried to work some of the circulation back into her own fingers she rued not having had the same foresight.

An excited yell pre-empted the first of the twins

emerging from a small copse of trees at the rear of the garden, closely followed by his sibling, a moment before he veered away and headed up a rickety ladder to a tree house. The girl took one look at her brother and then wandered across to a swing beneath another tree.

Annabelle looked up from her work and then propped the rake against the tree before resting her hands on her hips. 'Detective Hunter. What do you want? I'm trying to give my children a sense of normality after all the intrusions and stress.'

Kay waited until she'd reached the woman, and kept her voice low. 'Where's your husband, Annabelle?'

The woman used the heel of her hand to adjust her hat. 'At work.'

'I thought he would've rather been here to support you and the children at such a stressful time.'

'Yes, well I'm sure if he had an ordinary job he'd have done that. But he doesn't; he owns a company and is responsible for that and his employees.'

'When is he due back?'

Annabelle sighed. 'I don't know. Half past six, perhaps. Depends what happens, really – he's always at some client's beck and call.'

Barnes jerked his chin at the tree house as the boy

reappeared at the top of the ladder. 'How are they holding up?'

'As well as can be expected.'

'I'm surprised they still fit in there.'

'Christopher's the only one who uses it these days. Bethany grew out of it a while back. Says it's full of spiders.' A smile tugged at the woman's lips. 'Damien was the same at Christopher's age. Determined to stay in the tree house forever.'

'I think the height would put me off going up there,' said Kay.

Annabelle rolled her eyes. 'I told John and Damien they'd built it too high up.'

'How did Damien get on with his father?'

'Damien?' Annabelle reached out for the rake and began to sweep at the debris once more. 'All right, I suppose. As much as a father and son do. They had their disagreements from time to time, but that's to be expected. Damien grew up fast and had his own ambitions.'

'Did they argue much?'

'What do you mean?'

'Did they ever disagree about the business, or Damien's ambitions?'

Kay watched the other woman's expression cloud

over a moment before she gave her head a slight shake and forced a smile.

'I wouldn't know. They didn't discuss business things around me. I always insisted they kept that away from the table when we all used to sit down for dinner. Honestly, they were as bad as each other – never switched off.'

'How did John cope with the stress of running a business during the recession?'

Annabelle dropped the rake against the side of a small wooden shed. 'What's that supposed to mean?'

'The fight at the pub in Sutton Valence ten years ago. What was that all about?'

'I really can't remember.'

'Try.'

'Look, all right. John lost his temper with someone, that's all.'

'He was arrested, Annabelle. That's a bit more than simply losing his temper, isn't it?'

'He was provoked. The man accused him of owing money and started going on about how John was ruining local contractors' businesses because he wouldn't pay them. A lot of John's associates drank in that pub. He had to do something – he couldn't just let him carry on like that, ruining his reputation in front of everyone.'

'Was it true? Did John owe money?'

'Of course not. No more than anyone else does in this industry. Everything gets paid for eventually.'

'What about John's plans to hand over the business to Damien?' said Barnes.

Annabelle's chin jutted out. 'What do you mean?'

'Is John preparing to hand over a healthy business these days, or does he still have outstanding debts?'

'It-it's fine.'

'What are his plans for the business now?' said Kay.

'I don't bloody know. Like I said, he doesn't discuss business things around me. I don't want to hear about it anyway. I've got the twins to look after.'

On cue, the two teenagers came tearing across the garden to their mother, then slowed down as they approached, their expressions wary.

'Hello, you two,' said Barnes, smiling.

The girl gave a shy smile before she took off towards the house, her brother in tow.

'They're going to want something to eat,' said Annabelle. 'Was there anything else, or are we finished here?'

'Please let your husband know we need to speak to him as a matter of urgency,' said Kay. 'And that means today.'

FORTY-FIVE

'What do you mean, he's not at work?'

Kay spun her chair around and stalked towards Sharp's office, glaring at the different notices and memos from headquarters that littered one wall before moving to the window, her phone to her ear.

Carys's voice crackled as her mobile phone signal dipped out of range, then returned with a clarity that had Kay reaching for the volume control.

'They say he was in first thing this morning but they haven't seen him for nearly five hours, guv.'

'Where is he?'

'They don't know. He told them he had a meeting over near Tunbridge Wells but there's nothing in his diary. He was meant to see a client over an hour ago at Staplehurst, but he didn't show up for that. He's not answering his phone, either.'

'Shit.' Kay ran from the office and called across the incident room to Barnes. 'Get an alert out for John Brancourt and his car. Motorways, local airfields, the lot. Carys, you still there?'

'Guv.'

'I'll send a uniformed patrol over. Stay there in case Brancourt returns in the meantime. We'll get another lot over to his house.'

She ended the call and tossed her phone onto her desk.

'Guv? Malcolm Hodges is downstairs to see you,' said Gavin, slipping his jacket over his shoulders.

'Who?'

'The chap John Brancourt punched ten years ago. I spoke to him earlier today and asked him to come in. See if he can shed some light on Brancourt's business dealings, then and now.'

'Good work.'

Kay grabbed her jacket and followed Gavin from the room, easily keeping up with the lanky detective as he took the stairs at speed.

Malcolm Hodges rose from the plastic chair in reception as they entered, his pale blue eyes accentuated by wire-rimmed glasses. He unbuttoned a heavy woollen coat before shaking hands with them.

'Thanks for coming in,' said Gavin, steering the man towards an interview room and formally introducing them all for the purposes of recording the conversation. 'Please could you state your full name and occupation?'

'Malcolm Henry Hodges. I own a lighting installation company registered in Ashford.'

'How do you know John Brancourt?'

Hodges' top lip curled. 'I've had the unfortunate luck of being contracted by him some years ago. You know the outcome of that arrangement.'

'We know what's on record,' said Kay. 'Please could you tell us about it in your own words?'

'We won the work to provide some high specification spotlights for a retail fit out that Brancourt was managing over at Thanet. At the time, the fittings had to be shipped over from the States. The client was adamant that they wanted the best – it was a boutique music store, speakers, amplifiers, everything you might want for a home entertainment system. Money was no object as far as the client was concerned. Brancourt was a different matter. I tried to get a part payment up front, but he was having none of it. Said it'd be an insult to the client to ask. I'll be honest, I was nervous. You know what it was like ten years ago, businesses going under without a moment's notice.'

'What did you do?'

'Took the risk.' Hodges shrugged. 'Wasn't much else we could do. If we didn't supply the equipment, one of our competitors would've done.'

'So you did the job, and installed the lighting. Then what happened?' said Gavin.

'Brancourt didn't pay on time. This business is notoriously slow to pay anyway, which is why the contract gave us some protection with a sixty-day period for payments to be made. After three months of standard reminders from my accounts team and dropping subtle hints whenever I saw Brancourt in passing, I lost patience. I found out he'd been paid by the client but hadn't passed on the money to me, and I knew where he drank in the evening so I went to the pub to speak to him. You know what happened after that.'

'What did John say to you that night?'

'He told me that I'd pay for it if I took the matter to the courts, and said he'd make sure my company never worked in the area again. When I didn't back down, he punched me.'

'Did you ever get your money?' said Kay.

'Eventually. I had to take it to my solicitor though, and even then I had to threaten to remove my people and equipment from another site we were working on for Brancourt before anything happened.' Hodges tugged at his earlobe. 'I heard a rumour Brancourt was going to remove the equipment himself before I got a chance, but I think someone must've had a word with him because it never came to that.'

'Have you ever worked with John Brancourt since?'

'No, and I'm not the only one. John Brancourt has a habit of burning his bridges, Detective Hunter. I'm surprised he's still in business at all.'

CARYS APPEARED at the top of the stairs as Kay and Gavin returned from interviewing the lighting contractor, her face glum.

'Still no sign of John Brancourt,' she said, falling into step with them as they entered the incident room. She jerked her thumb towards the window at the darkening sky. 'It's getting colder out there, too.'

'Did you look into his finances with Amanda?'

Carys held up a sheaf of documents. 'He's hanging in there at the moment, but we found a slew of historical County Court Judgments against his business from ten years ago. He might've paid everyone eventually, but they had to take him in front of the magistrates to get anywhere. I don't think they'd have seen their money otherwise.'

'Let's work on what we've got while we're waiting to hear where he is,' said Kay. 'Are uniform helping with the search?'

'There are half a dozen local patrols searching his known haunts, guv. I've spoken to his wife and she's given us a list of places he might be. She's obviously worried. She said it's completely out of character for him to simply vanish like this.'

Kay filled a cup with water from the dispenser next to the window and wandered across to the whiteboard, the noise from the team diminishing as they hovered around her, an air of expectancy filling the space. She turned to face them.

'Speaking to the contractor Brancourt assaulted ten years ago, it seems Damien's father has a history of not paying his suppliers and taking other people's equipment if he can't get the money together in time to stop them recovering anything. That makes think it wasn't Damien's idea to steal the copper wire from the Petersham Building, but John's.'

Gavin frowned. 'I wonder how he persuaded him

to do that? Damien had no interest in his dad's business – that's what Alexander Hill told us, right? So, why would he help him?'

'I don't know. A sense of family loyalty, perhaps?'

'I can't see it, guv,' said Barnes. 'I can't imagine John driving Damien towards Maidstone to catch his train and then saying "oh, by the way, son, do you mind if we drop in and nick some copper wire before you go on holiday".'

Murmured laughter followed his suggestion, and Kay held up her hand to silence the team.

'When you put it like that it does seem far-fetched, but what if Damien had a reason to agree to it?'

Carys glanced down as her mobile phone began to ring.

'Get it,' said Kay.

She waited while the detective constable spoke in a low tone before giving Kay the thumbs up.

'We've got John Brancourt,' she said. 'He's been spotted near the weir at Lee Road in Yalding.'

Barnes took one look at the rain beating against the windows, then turned back to Kay. 'In this weather, they'll have to consider opening the sluice gates to stop the reservoir from flooding.'

Kay was already moving to where her jacket was hanging on the back of her chair. 'We need to get over there. We can't have John doing anything stupid.'

'Do you think he might?' said Barnes, catching the car keys Carys tossed to him and following Kay out of the door.

'He's desperate,' she said. 'And guilty. I don't know what he's thinking right now, but it can't be good.'

They began to run.

FORTY-SIX

The blue lights from two patrol cars were arcing across the night sky by the time Kay and Barnes tore through the village to reach the stone bridge across the River Medway.

One patrol car had been driven over the other side of the bridge and sat parked outside the pub on the opposite bank to block traffic travelling from the railway station.

Although it was after midnight, there were still half a dozen cars corralled by the officers and the frustration of the motorists keen to get home was palpable even from where Kay stood, as one by one they were instructed to reverse and then find an alternative route.

She marched towards the nearest constable and

held up her warrant card in the beam from his torch. 'Where is he?'

'Just past the safety gates, guv. A woman from the cottage over there called it in. I recognised him when we got here. The pub closed an hour ago, thank goodness.'

'Thanks.' Kay agreed with his sentiment. They didn't need a bunch of inebriated regulars gawking at the scene. She peered over the rampart. 'Is there a way down there?'

The constable turned and swept his torch beam across the path. 'That's the only route down to the river bank, through the car park. The other side is a sheer drop and was fenced off a few years ago.'

Kay squinted into the darkness beyond, then pointed to the smaller bridge above the weir gates where John Brancourt stood as if mesmerised by the water. 'And that goes over to Teapot Island, yes?'

'Yes, guv. There's a third patrol over there keeping the marina residents away from the bridge.'

'How the hell did he get through the safety gates and onto the bridge?'

'Bolt cutters, I presume, guv. His work van is parked over there. I was down here for lunch at the pub over the summer and there were bloody great padlocks on the gates back then.'

'Okay, good work. Barnes, let's have a wander down there and see if we can talk some sense into Brancourt. We'll avoid the gate for now in case he panics with us being that close.'

It took them longer than Kay anticipated to reach the water's edge, the grass slippery under their feet from the rainfall that soaked the landscape. Once she was sure she wasn't going to fall in, Kay shielded her eyes and squinted at the bridge in the distance.

'What's he playing at then?' she said. She brought her hands to her mouth and called out. 'John. Why don't you walk back to the path and we'll have a talk? Does that sound like a good idea to you?'

In response, Brancourt rested his hands on the metal barrier and leaned forward, staring at the water.

Barnes jerked his chin at the dark water. 'He'd break his neck jumping into that. It's too shallow. At best, he'd break his legs.'

'And there are hidden currents. Look, you can see the way the water eddies.'

She watched the circling pool as it flowed past their position before disappearing underneath the arches of the bridge, lapping at the stone pillars and then shooting out the other side.

A roaring suddenly cut through the air, and Kay spun around to see the weir gates begin to rise, releasing water from the top pool in a cascading plume that bellowed through the night air as it dropped into the shallows.

'Back!' said Barnes, grasping her hand and pulling her away from the water's edge.

Their feet slid into the soft mud of the riverbank as they tried to hurry away from the flow, white foam spewing from the concrete and steel sluice gates.

Kay tightened her grip on Barnes as her boots sank into the ground, throwing her off-balance as she fought against a rising tide of panic that engulfed her.

The water level was already lapping at her heels.

'Give me your other hand.'

She reached out blindly, her fingertips brushing against his before finding air, and then a moment later he had hold of her, dragging her out of the mud inch by inch.

'Shit,' said Kay as Barnes pulled her up to the asphalt path above the river. She looked down at the swirling angry water. 'Who the hell did that?'

'They're automatic. As soon as the pool up here reaches a certain level, the gates open. It's why there were some near drownings with kids getting caught out last summer. No-one takes any notice of all the bloody signs up here.'

'Where's John?'

'Over there.'

She looked to where he pointed, and gasped as the man began to climb over the safety railing above the weir gates.

Walking as fast as she dared, she moved from the grassy bank to the bridge, drew closer to the security gate and then paused. She removed an elastic from her wrist and tied her hair back, then squinted at Barnes through the horizontal rain that lashed at the bridge.

His expression was incredulous.

'You're not seriously thinking of jumping in to save him if he goes in, guv?' He peered over the railing at the raging torrent below. 'That's going through there at something like ten tonnes per second.'

'We can't let him hurt himself.'

'Guv, if he jumps in he's going to be dead in seconds. So are you.'

Kay gritted her teeth.

Beyond their position, she could see the outline of John Brancourt wavering at the edge of the railing as if transfixed by the churning water.

'I've got to try something. Stay here. Don't let anyone come through this gate unless I call for help – or we go in the water.'

Without waiting for a response, she slipped through the gap and shoved her hands in her pockets and headed towards Brancourt hoping she exuded an air of nonchalance.

Her heart rate skipped a beat.

She'd only had to deal with one suicidal case before in her police career, and the memory of that threatened to surface again, all too clear in her mind.

She gave her head a shake to clear the thought, inhaled the cold clear night air, and squared her shoulders.

She stopped a few paces from John, aware that he'd seen her but hadn't moved.

It gave her hope.

'Good grief, John. It's freezing up here.' Kay took in the steep drop, then turned back to Brancourt. 'What are you doing? Annabelle's worried sick about you.'

'I used to bring him fishing here when he was a kid,' he said. 'Loved it. 'Course, that was before all these safety barriers were up. Didn't need them back then. We used to look out for each other.'

Kay tried to ignore the biting wind that nipped at her wet clothing. 'What happened, John?'

In reply, he shook his head.

'Did you argue?'

He shifted his weight, and Kay fought down the bile that rose in her stomach.

'John, please – for the sake of the twins and Annabelle.'

He lowered his chin, droplets of rain running down his face and dripping off the end of his nose.

Such was the ferocity of the downpour, it took a moment for Kay to realise the man was crying. In two steps, she was beside him, her hand on his arm.

'John, whatever it is you've done, this won't help. This won't give your family the answers they need. Don't do this. Please.'

He sagged against her weight, and she reached out to draw him to safety, shivering as she coaxed him over the metal barrier, and then signalled to Barnes and a uniformed officer to help her before she turned back to Brancourt.

'Come on. Let's get you somewhere warm and dry. It's time we had a talk.'

FORTY-SEVEN

Barnes ensured the heater was turned on full blast while they followed the red tail lights of the patrol car racing towards Maidstone with John Brancourt inside, the steam from their wet clothes fogging up the windscreen.

Kay insisted he go home and dry off as soon as he dropped her at the station, and then found Gavin and Carys waiting for her in the incident room, armed with a bottle of brandy left over from the Christmas party that they'd found shoved at the back of a filing cabinet.

'Are you all right?'

Kay turned at Sharp's voice, his concern palpable as he ran his eyes over her wet hair and soaked clothing.

She nodded in reply, not yet certain her teeth wouldn't chatter if she tried to answer despite the nip of brandy she'd had, and then snuggled her shoulders deeper into the thick woollen blanket that Hughes had located in the first aid locker.

She ignored the sweet tea Gavin had placed beside her, too scared she would burn her numb fingers on the hot china mug. Beside her, her ankle boots left pools of water on the carpet, the scrunched up newspaper that had been placed inside each not yet taking effect.

Sharp's shoulders relaxed and he handed her a canvas tote bag. 'I took the liberty of going around to your house and asking Adam to put together some dry clothes for you. Go have a hot shower downstairs and be ready in twenty minutes to interview John Brancourt. I take it you want to be present?'

'I do. Thanks, guv.'

'No problem.' He winked. 'Although I should warn you, you've got some explaining to do when you get home.'

'I'll bet I have.'

'Go on – before you catch pneumonia or something.'

Kay didn't wait to be told twice. She risked a sip of the tea before heading downstairs to the women's changing room, careful not to sneeze until the door was firmly locked behind her for fear of causing her colleagues further alarm.

Stripping off her wet clothes, she pulled a clean pair of suit trousers, a cashmere jumper and a long-sleeved cotton top from the tote bag and hung them over the radiator to warm, and then unzipped the vanity bag Adam had packed and pulled out shampoo and soap.

She wasn't a fan of the showers at work and often thought them draughty and in need of retiling, but thirty seconds after standing under the steaming water she sighed with pleasure.

A tingling sensation began in her toes and worked its way up her body as her circulation began to warm her extremities and she sighed with relief as she dried and dressed.

Pulling the jumper over her head, she tied back her hair and applied a little make-up, and then took a moment to sit on the bench and gather her thoughts.

'Bloody families,' she muttered.

SHARP FINISHED GIVING Carys and Gavin

instructions in the observation suite and then turned to Kay and raised an eyebrow.

'Shall we?'

She nodded in reply, and followed him along the corridor to the interview room.

Kay had seen plenty of broken men in her time, but none had filled her with the same sense of melancholy she felt as she took a seat opposite the solicitor and looked across at his client.

Sergeant Hughes had ensured John Brancourt received the benefit of a hot shower and a change of clothes while the team had waited for his solicitor to arrive, and now the accused sat on one side of the metal table with his hands wrapped around a steaming cup of coffee, his eyes downcast.

She recited the formal caution, but wasted no time on niceties.

'I'm tired of being lied to, John. Every time we've talked over the past three weeks you've sprung another surprise on me. You hold back information in the deluded sense it's going to protect you.'

'I'm trying to protect my business. I need to look after my family.'

She spun the laptop screen to face Brancourt. 'This is CCTV footage from the Sittingbourne Road for the night Damien disappeared,' she said. 'In addition to this, I've had a team of officers reviewing footage at Heathrow for the twenty-four hours before Damien's flight. That's five terminals, the car parks, the drop-off points and the airport lounges, but there's no sign of Damien. He never made it to Heathrow. He never caught a train from Maidstone East.'

She smacked the laptop shut, and Brancourt jerked backwards.

'What happened, John?'

Brancourt continued to stare at the table.

Kay fought back her impatience. 'Must've been a hell of a shock when you found out he was talking to Hill about a job offer.'

'I didn't know until you told me. He kept it a secret.'

'I thought you and Damien didn't have secrets.'

Brancourt shifted in his seat and then stared at the coffee growing cold in the mug he held, but said nothing.

'Why did Damien change his mind about taking over the family business?'

This time, Brancourt's eyes met her gaze and she could see the depth of sorrow that wracked him.

'He told me when I dropped him off that night that he'd never work for me again.'

'Why?'

'I owe a lot of favours.'

'We got that impression. The business isn't doing as well as you've been telling us, is it?'

Brancourt choked out a bitter laugh. 'You don't know the half of it.'

'Tell me.'

'I can't.'

'John, if you don't tell us who's threatening you, we can't help.'

'I know.' He pushed the coffee mug away, and slumped back in his seat. 'It's my own fault. I messed people around, didn't pay them when I should've done. In the end, none of the legitimate contractors would work with me. I was left with the dregs.'

'You still had choices, John. You didn't have to employ criminals.'

'I've got two more kids to put through university. I can't help with their education if the business goes under, can I?'

'You've only got yourself to blame for the state of your business,' said Sharp. 'No-one else.'

'Did you steal the fibre optic cabling that went missing?' said Kay.

He shrugged. 'Yes.'

'But you sourced some new cabling when Alex Hill found out it had gone and the schedule was at risk. How did you benefit from the theft if you had to end up replacing it?'

'Because I got it dirt cheap. I made a profit.' He blinked. 'It all helped. Anything I could scrimp and save, I put into paying off my debts.'

'You didn't scrimp and save, John. You stole from honest, hard-working people.' Kay turned a page in the folder. 'Is that why you went back to steal the copper wire as well?'

Brancourt frowned. 'I never stole any copper wiring. I couldn't, even if I wanted to. It was still live.'

'On the bridge tonight, you reminisced about the times you'd spent with Damien as a child. You gave me the impression you actually gave a shit about your family. Those weren't tears of grief were they, John? That was the knowledge that you'd been found out. That was the knowledge it was all over. That was fear.'

'I had nothing to do with Damien's death.'

'Where did you take him?'

'Look. Maybe I didn't tell you the whole story.' His eyes shifted to the left, then back. 'We had an early dinner at home. All of us. I was meant to be dropping Damien off at the station, and then Christopher asked if he could come along as well.

He likes going to the arcade place in the town centre.'

'He's under age.'

'He's tall for his age.'

'So, you dropped them both off...'

'Behind the Petersham Building. It was closer to the arcade, see?'

'Was Christopher the "friend" you mentioned?'

'Yes.'

'Why lie to us?'

'I knew he was gambling. I didn't want him to get into trouble. It's just a bit of fun for him, see?'

'Then what happened?'

'Nothing. I dropped them off, and then went home.'

'How did Christopher get home?'

'Bus, I suppose.'

'You suppose? What time did he get in?'

'I don't know. About eleven, I think. I'm not sure.'

Exasperated, Sharp pulled the photograph of Damien's mummified body from the file and thrust it at Brancourt. 'We're trying to find the answers to why your son was electrocuted while stealing copper wire, John. We're trying to find out who stuffed his body into a ceiling cavity and then hid his bag.'

Brancourt ran a shaking hand over the photograph. 'No. No…'

Alarmed, Kay looked at Sharp and then back to Brancourt. 'John? John, what is it?'

'Christopher,' he whispered. 'What have you done?'

FORTY-EIGHT

'I don't understand.'

Annabelle Brancourt tore at the paper tissue between her fingers and shook her head. 'This can't be happening.'

'We need to speak to Christopher, Mrs Brancourt. Now.'

Kay ran her eyes over the glossy magazine that lay open on the kitchen table, its staged photographs depicting a perfect life that was impossible for many.

She ignored the two uniformed officers who hovered at the door, their radios crackling, and pulled out a chair next to the woman. 'We've been speaking with John at the police station, Annabelle. He's confirmed he took Christopher with him when he gave Damien a lift to the train station last June.'

'That doesn't mean anything.'

'Maybe not, but we do need to eliminate Christopher from our enquiries.'

'No, that's not right. He idolised Damien.'

'We think that's why he went to the Petersham Building with him,' said Kay. 'Damien never planned to go to Nepal, Annabelle. It was all a ruse from the start. He wanted a clean break, and he needed money for capital.'

'You mean he didn't want to be with us?'

'He didn't want the responsibility for taking over the business. Not after what John had done to it. He didn't believe there was a future for him in it, and he was trying to distance himself from the family name. It's why he'd been speaking to Alexander Hill about a job. That was probably one of many schemes he was contemplating to try and start out on his own.'

Annabelle dabbed at mascara-streaked eyes, then reached out and wound her fingers around the stem of her half-empty wine glass.

'He always was an ungrateful sod,' she said.

She drained the remaining red in one gulp, and then placed the glass back on the table with such force that the stem shattered between her fingers.

Kay took one look at the blood bubbling from the

cuts and pushed her chair backwards. 'Carys – towel. Hanging up on the front of the oven.'

She reached out for Annabelle's hand, turning it gently so she could assess the damage.

'You're lucky. They're superficial cuts.' Taking the towel Carys held out to her, she wrapped it around the woman's hand. 'Keep your hand up in the air for a bit to stem the flow. I don't think you're going to need stitches.'

'Thank you.'

'Where is Christopher now?'

'Upstairs, in his bedroom of course.'

'You need to show me.'

Annabelle clutched the towel around her hand and shoved her chair backwards. 'Come on, then.'

She led the way out to the hallway and then up the flight of stairs to a wide landing.

As Kay reached the top step, a door at the back of the house opened and Bethany peered out, her eyes wide.

'What's going on, Mum?'

'Nothing. Go back to bed.'

'Where's Dad?'

'Busy.'

Bethany paused for a moment, then turned away, leaving the door open a crack.

'Which one is Christopher's room?'

'This one. At the front.'

Annabelle crossed the thick carpet and knocked on the door. 'Christopher? The police are here.'

Carys raised an eyebrow at Kay in the silence that followed.

'Christopher?'

Annabelle knocked once more, and then twisted the door knob and flipped the light switch.

Kay took one look at the woman's surprised expression and spun on her heel.

As she raced across the landing, Bethany appeared, a thick dressing gown over her pyjamas.

'He's outside,' she said.

'Outside?'

Her mother's shrill response made the teenager wince.

'I saw him.'

'Where did he go, Bethany?' Kay kept her voice soft, unwilling to alarm the girl any further.

'Down the garden. I saw him out the window.'

'Carys, with me.'

She shot down the stairs, rounded the newel post without stopping and beckoned to the two officers.

'Give me a torch. Stay there in case he comes back. We're heading out to the garden.'

She heard the muffled "ma'am" as she wrenched open the front door, and then ran along the gravelled path to the back garden, the landscape unfamiliar in the darkness.

'Where do you think he went?' said Carys.

Kay traced the border of the property, her eyes following a large hedgerow that ran from the house and down the right hand side until it petered out near the copse of trees.

She began walking towards the wooded area, and then stopped at the base of the large oak tree and raised her chin.

Above her, up a ladder that looked as if it would fall apart at any moment, was the tree house.

'He's up there,' Kay murmured.

Carys craned her neck to follow her gaze, and then took a step back. 'Are you going up?'

'I'd better. Wait here.'

She tucked the torch into the collar of her jacket, gripped the sides of the ladder, and began to climb.

It was higher than she thought.

By the time she reached the top, the wind whipped at her hair and buffeted her against the floor of the tree house.

She pulled out the torch and swept it around the wooden hideaway.

Coal-black eyes stared out of the gloom at her, and she lowered the beam.

'Christopher?'

'He ruined it,' said the teenager, his voice full of anger. 'He ruined everything.'

The ladder wobbled under Kay's weight and she held her breath, refusing to look down. If the flimsy framework collapsed, she'd have no way to break the fall.

'Was it Damien's idea to steal the copper wire?' she said.

'Of course it was. I didn't even know it was there.'

'Why did you go?'

'Because he asked me to.' Christopher's voice took on a desperate tone.

'And you'd do anything for your brother, wouldn't you?' she said.

'Yes.'

It was little more than a whisper.

'Your mum's really worried about you.'

'She never liked Damien.'

Kay grabbed hold of the top of the ladder, his admission catching her off guard.

'Didn't she?'

There was movement in the shadows, and then Christopher appeared.

'You need to be careful. Dad was meant to fix this ladder last summer.'

'Thanks.'

He shrugged and looked away; a shy tic that broke her heart.

She took the opportunity to hoist herself into the tree house, placed her torch on the floor then turned around and concentrated on the view.

Beyond the woods, the sun was beginning to crest the horizon.

'Why didn't your mum like Damien, then?'

'She said he was ungrateful.'

'Was he?'

'No. He was only pissed off because Dad kept screwing things up with the business.'

'Is that why he didn't want to take it over?'

'Yeah. Said it was worthless. No-one wants to work with Dad as it is. Nobody respectable, anyway.'

'Were you getting bullied at school?'

Christopher drew his knees up to his chin and stared at the floor. 'Dad always forgets that when he does something, it makes all of us look bad, too. Bethany gets into trouble at school because they're always picking on her. Girls are worse than the boys. Even Mum was affected. She used to like playing badminton at a club with her friends until about two years ago. She had to quit because Dad owed her friends' husbands money.'

'How did Damien know about the copper wiring?'

'He used to go along to the site meetings with Dad.'

'How'd you get into the place? It had a security company looking after it.'

'Turns out Dad wasn't the only one cutting costs. When we got there, there was nobody around.'

'No security guards?'

'No. I guess they were skimming off the profits as well.'

Kay swivelled herself around so she was facing Christopher in the low light from the torch.

'How did you get in?'

'Damien had a spare key. He must've got it cut without Dad finding out. I asked, but he wouldn't tell me. He was angry with me by then.'

'Why?'

'Because I wanted to know who he was going to sell the copper wire to. He told me to stop asking so many questions.'

'Did he hit you?'

Christopher lowered his eyes, and then nodded.

Kay sighed. 'What happened when you removed the underlay to get to the copper wire?

Christopher swallowed, his face devoid of any colour. 'Damien pulled the boards up. We weren't talking much by then. I think he was wishing he hadn't asked me to help him. I don't think he was paying attention. When we first got into the building, he'd told me not to press any of the light switches because the power was on.' He shivered. 'I turned my back – only for a second. I was looking for another torch so we could see into the gap.'

A solitary tear ran over his cheek. 'I thought I'd reminded him about the power, really I did.'

'What happened next?' said Kay.

Christopher used his shirt sleeve to wipe at his eyes. 'There was a sound. Like a gasp, then a thud. All the power went off. I just stood there. I don't know how long for. I was too scared to turn around and look. And then I realised I had to move. I had to do something.'

'You covered up the death of your own brother,' said Kay.

Christopher nodded.

'Why didn't you report it?' she said. 'Why did you hide his body?'

'Because I panicked. I didn't know what else to

do. He-he was dead, there was no power in the building, and so I dragged Damien across the floor until he fell inside the cavity and sealed it back up.'

'What were you planning to do in April when he didn't show up?'

'I suppose he could've gone missing out there. People do, all the time, don't they? Just disappear without a trace.'

'What did you do with his bag?'

In reply, a scraping sound reached her ears as he turned and pulled a canvas holdall from the corner of the tree house.

'He told me to hang on to it while he went and bought some cigarettes before we went into the building,' he said.

'Didn't your sister wonder why it was here?'

'Bethany doesn't come up here anymore.'

'Why not?'

'I told her the place was infested with spiders.'

Kay swallowed. 'Is it?'

'No. I only told her that to keep her out of here.' He rested a hand on the bag. 'I didn't know what else to do with this.'

'Shove it over here.'

Kay stopped the bag with one hand, and then unzipped it and shone her torch inside.

Copper wire glinted in the light from the beam, and as she delved underneath it, she pulled out a passport.

'You didn't sell the copper wire.'

'No.'

Kay re-zipped the bag. 'Look, I'm not too good with heights,' she said. 'Do you mind if we finish this conversation somewhere at ground level?'

'Am I in trouble?'

'I'm not going to lie to you. I'll do what I can, but—'

She watched as he shuffled awkwardly across the planks of wood that made up the floor of the tree house and then pushed his legs out in front of him.

'I didn't mean to. I was scared.'

'I know you were. Now, do you mind showing me the best way to get down from here? I really wasn't kidding about the heights thing.'

Five minutes later, Kay stood at the base of the tree as a uniformed officer led Christopher across the lawn towards the driveway where a patrol car waited.

'What will happen to him?' Annabelle called out from where she stood next to Carys.

Kay joined them. 'I told Christopher I'd do what I can, Mrs Brancourt, but it's possible the Crown Prosecution Service might pursue a charge for involuntary manslaughter. There's also the matter of hiding Damien's body – the charge they'll likely raise is called denying the coroner a body. Depending on how they view the circumstances leading up to Damien's death, they may well charge him with attempted theft as well.'

'Two sons,' whispered Annabelle. 'Now who will John pass the business on to? We'll be finished.'

Kay's attention was caught by movement at a window on the ground floor of the house, a curtain dropping back into place.

'You have a daughter,' she said. 'Maybe once this is all over you could have a think about breaking with tradition and passing it on to her.'

Annabelle wrapped her coat around her shoulders and kicked at a loose stone in the path. 'Do you have a daughter, Detective Hunter?'

Kay turned so the other woman couldn't see her face, and then began to walk away.

'No,' she said. 'I lost her.'

FORTY-NINE

Kay climbed from the passenger seat of Adam's four-wheel drive vehicle, the wind whipping her hair into her face and making her eyes sting.

The next gust flushed out the sound of bells from the small church in Shepway, celebrating the mid-morning wedding service they had passed on the way.

She'd received a phone call from Barnes an hour ago, updating her from the incident room with the news that the Crown Prosecution Service had confirmed they would be charging Christopher Brancourt for concealing the truth about his brother's death, and that Sharp had sent the remainder of the team home for the weekend to ensure they were fully rested before what was expected to be a busy week ahead while they pursued an investigation into Mark Sutton's business affairs.

'Take the day off, Kay,' he'd said. 'I've got it under control. Spend some time with Adam – you've hardly seen each other these past few weeks what with this case and everything else.'

Kay had tried to argue with him, but the detective sergeant was having none of it. She smiled at the memory – Barnes was a good friend, and she respected him as a colleague, too.

And, she had to admit, he had a fair point.

She slammed the door as Adam joined her, a bouquet of flowers in his hand.

'Take these, I'll get the secateurs,' he said.

She inhaled the sweet scent from the brightly coloured carnations as Adam rummaged under the seats before extracting himself and locking the doors.

'Shall we?' He wrapped his fingers around hers and chuckled under his breath. 'Freezing cold, as always.'

'I should've worn gloves.'

Despite the mid-morning hour, her breath fogged as she fell into step beside Adam, their boots crunching on the gravelled surface of the car park. Weak sunlight gave the sky a washed-out hue and

Kay shivered as she tugged her scarf up over her coat collar to shield herself from the chill breeze.

Adam's thick black hair ruffled in the wind, and for a moment she fell silent, content in his company and relieved that he was here to accompany her.

She knew she wouldn't be able to do this on her own, not today.

The grief ebbed and flowed within her, a dull ache that clutched at her chest on some days and reduced to a steady hum the rest of the time. She accepted that it would never fade completely, and in fact dreaded the thought that she would ever stop feeling the pain.

As if sensing her thoughts, Adam squeezed her hand, the warmth from his fingers enveloping her.

He said nothing, the words unnecessary.

When she had recovered, when she had first returned to work to find herself thrust into a nightmare of a pursuit to find a killer before another teenage girl died, he had finally told her what had happened.

Kay had pushed the less painful memories away, and the rest were lost to a mind that refused to contemplate what might have been.

Adam, on the other hand, had been the one holding her hand in the back of the ambulance, refusing to let the emergency workers take her away without him.

Adam had been the one who had curled up on the floor of the hospital waiting room, exhausted and unsure whether his partner and child would live.

Adam had been the one who had collapsed with relief tainted with a desolation that had wracked him for months when the surgeon had found him at three in the morning to tell him Kay had lived, but their daughter had not.

In time, they had healed together, the loss of their daughter a burden they had borne like so many other families before them.

Kay stopped in her tracks, pulling Adam to a sudden standstill.

He turned to face her. 'What is it?'

She stood on tiptoe and kissed him. 'Love you.'

He pulled her into a hug, burying his face in her hair. 'Love you, too.'

She pulled away, wiped at her stinging eyes, then reached for his hand once more. 'Come on.'

The colder weather had stunted the growth of the cemetery's lawn, and a path was easily found between the stone markers of loved ones lost to time.

Kay held her breath as she drew nearer, the weight

on her chest wrapping its way around her heart as the plain stone of her daughter's grave came into view.

The council-employed gardeners had kept the weeds at bay and removed the spent stems from previous bouquets, and Adam bent to pull out an errant clump of couch grass that obscured her name.

Elizabeth Hunter-Turner.

'I'll fill this up with water,' said Adam, holding the metal vase that had been at the head of the grave. 'Will you be all right on your own for a moment?'

'Yes.'

She gave a small smile as he walked away towards a standpipe at the end of the line of headstones, then turned back to her daughter's grave.

'Hello, Lizzy.'

A ragged sigh escaped her lips as she crouched beside the stone and ran her hands over the smooth surface.

She wondered what it would have been like to run her hand over her daughter's hands, what it would have been like to brush her hair, the fun they would have had as a family.

Instead, she and Adam were bereft; childless.

'God, it hurts,' she whispered.

She sniffed as the sound of footsteps reached her,

and then Adam crouched beside her and replaced the now-full vase on its base.

He gave her a gentle nudge. 'I've seen what you're like with knives. Do you want me to cut the flowers?'

Kay choked out a laugh. 'Yes. Go on.'

She removed the elastic band from the stems and held them out to him while he snipped at the ends and then between them they arranged the flowers, working in silence.

When it was done, Adam pulled her to her feet and wrapped his arms around her.

Kay snuggled into the warmth of his chest, grateful for his closeness.

'We're going to be all right, Kay,' he said. 'We're going to be all right.'

THE END

Dear Reader,

Thank you for picking up a copy of *Bridge to Burn* to read. I hope you enjoyed the story.

If you enjoyed reading *Bridge to Burn*, I'd be grateful if you could write a review. It doesn't have to be long, just a few words, but it is often the way that new readers discover one of my books for the first time.

If you'd like to stay up to date with my new releases as well as exclusive competitions and giveaways, please join my Reader Group at my website, www.rachelamphlett.com. I will never share your email address, and you can unsubscribe at any time.

You can also contact me via Facebook, Twitter, or by email via the contact page on my website. I love hearing from readers – I read every message and will always reply.

Thanks again for your support.

Best wishes,

Rachel Amphlett

.

Printed in Great Britain
by Amazon

56919541R00213